Still the Shadows

Elizabeth Fields

ISBN-13: 978-0692290057
ISBN-10: 0692290052

Contents

Flypaper

"You hardly eat at all these days, dear." Jameson looked lovingly across the dinner table at his wife of twenty-four years.

She stared straight ahead with a blank expression. He realized at that moment that he hadn't seen her smile in quite some time. He thought back to the last time he heard her laugh or saw a grin spread across this face he loved so dearly, and he decided it had been even longer than he'd thought. She hadn't quite been the same since the accident. Nothing had been quite the same since that day, but he loved her, and so he did his very best to keep her in good spirits.

"Well, darling," he said taking her hand in his, "you seem very tired. Perhaps we should call it a night. I'll get you upstairs."

She didn't respond. He knew her well enough to know this meant she agreed. If she didn't want to do something, she'd never been shy about voicing her opinion before.

He went to her side and slid her chair out a bit so he could get a good grip on her. Since the accident, she hadn't been able to get up the stairs herself. She hadn't been able to do much of anything at all herself. Jameson had to take care of her. He didn't mind it. He actually enjoyed taking care of his bride. He wouldn't have had it any other way. He lifted her up and held her close to him. She felt a tad lighter than she had in the days before.

"We've got to get you eating, my love." He held her tight and walked her gently up the stairs and into their room. He laid her down on the bed they'd shared for almost a quarter of a century and gently kissed her on the forehead.

"Sleep well, my angel," he said sweetly. She didn't say a word back, but he knew she appreciated the sentiment. He knew she loved him, and that was all he needed.

***

Amy found the morning sun unbearably bright. She shielded her eyes from the beams that seemed directed right at her. Even with her hand covering them, her eyes started to tear up. She looked around and noticed waves of heat rising from the hot asphalt behind them.

"This is just perfect, Jake," she scolded her boyfriend. "Who the hell plans a road trip and doesn't think to bring a spare?"

"I forgot, okay?" Jake was inspecting a mangled tire on the side of his SUV.

Amy held her cell phone up in the air and twirled herself around, trying to get a signal.

"Nothing! Shit! Give me yours." She waved her hand at him impatiently.

"Good luck," he said, sighing. He already knew his service wouldn't be any better. They had the same carrier, and neither of them had had any service for the last thirty miles.

She snatched the phone from his hand and twirled around with it in the air the same way she had with hers.

"Damn it, Jake!"

"Calm down," he said carefully. "I'm sorry, okay. What else do you want from me?" He was clearly frustrated with the situation.

"Where the hell did your spare go anyway?"

"I don't know! I've never had to use it. Maybe someone stole it. You never know." He knew exactly where his spare tire went, but he wasn't going to tell Amy. He had given it to his brother, Gabe, just a few weeks earlier. Gabe had a flat and called Jake to come help him out. Jake's spare just happened to fit Gabe's truck, and he was supposed to get the tire repaired and bring back the spare, but in true Gabe fashion, he did not. He also borrowed seventy dollars to get his tire fixed, and Jake hadn't seen a return on that yet either. Jake knew it wouldn't cost seventy dollars to get a hole patched up, but he lent it to him anyway. Amy despised Gabe. She thought he was a drunken, loser leech, and she couldn't stand how Jake always came to his rescue. At this moment, seeing how angry she was already, he knew better than to tell her why they had gone on their cross-state trip sans spare tire.

"Look," Jake said, "I'm sorry. I really am, but there really isn't much we can do about it now, is there?" He walked toward his angry girlfriend. He placed his hand on her right hip. "Babe," he said sweetly, "I'm sorry."

She groaned in protest.

"Come on," he continued, "forgive me? Please?" He went in for a kiss. She batted him away. "We're out here in the middle of nowhere... why don't we make good use of this time alone?" he suggested.

"Yeah, right, buddy," she said, laughing.

He stuck out his bottom lip and whined, "am I forgiven?"

"Ugh!" She resigned. "Fine! But get away from me; it's too hot." She gave him a quick kiss, pushed him playfully away from her and then looked around desperately in both directions. "So, genius, what now?"

"Well... I'm thinking we walk."

"Walk? Yeah, okay. Sure. You go that way, and I'll be right here waiting for you." The idea of spending one more second in the heat made upset her.

"Come on. It'll be a fun adventure. We'll discover new lands."

"Okay, fine, Magellan. Which way do you propose we go?" She looked again in both directions. The blurry lines rose angrily from the asphalt. It made her eyes hurt to look at them wriggle their way up toward the sky.

"Well," he said, looking around, "according to the map, we're about eight miles from the nearest town, so maybe we should go back."

"Back where? There's nothing behind us." Amy looked down and swatted a fly from her leg. She groaned again, annoyed. If there was anything she hated more than heat, it was flies.

"Yeah, remember? We passed that farmhouse about a mile or so back, and you were like *oh what a pretty pony* or something like that. Maybe they have a phone we can use."

"Uh, yeah, I believe I said *hey look a horse*, but I'm not so sure about going up to a stranger's house and asking if we can use their phone. Isn't that rude?" She swatted at the air, fervently. The fly was pretty persistent.

"Normally, I'd say it's a good rule not to drop in on strangers and ask for favors, but we're kind of in a tight spot here. Come on, babe. Whatta ya say?" Jake asked.

He looked at her with his gorgeous blue eyes. She wondered why he wasn't wearing sunglasses. It was way too bright for no sunglasses. After that thought passed came a feeling of surrender. She could rarely resist a plea when he looked at her this way. He knew it, too, and he often used it to his advantage.

"Fine! God! I am so over this trip already. I hate the heat. I hate flies. I hate dirt!" She complained.

"Oh come on, you love the heat. You'll get a darker tan," he said.

"I go to tanning beds for a reason. You're in, you're out, and no tan lines. I am so gonna get tan lines on this little adventure hike. How sexy. I'll look like I'm wearing a tank top and shorts when I'm naked."

"Ooh," Jake said, followed by a purring sound. "That is sexy. I can't wait to see that."

"Shut up," she said, laughing. "Let's go."

"Okay." Jake grabbed their water bottles from the car, put on his sunglasses, and hit the lock button on his clicker. The car honked twice at them as they walked away from it.

Amy looked back at the car, missing its air conditioning. She made a whimper.

"It'll be fine. You'll live," Jake said.

"I know, but she looks so sad back there all by herself."

"Himself," Jake corrected.

She laughed, and the two of them continued their trek down the super-hot highway. Not a single car passed as they walked. They tried to keep a steady pace, but the heat bore down on them. Twenty minutes later, they were drenched with sweat, halfway through their waters, and almost to the farmhouse.

"There!" Jake said excitedly. "It's just up ahead."

"Great. Hope they're home after all this," Amy said.

"Funny, Aims," Jake said.

"Nope, not funny; just our luck." She lightly jabbed him in the side with her elbow. They laughed, but they were both nervous that nobody would be home, or worse no one would want to help them.

"Well," Jake said, "best case scenario, these people are angels, and they'll save us and get us on our way. Worst case, maybe you get to pet a pony."

"It's a horse, and yes, I think I would like to meet him." She took a giant swig from her water bottle and let out a tired sigh.

Amy worked out almost every day and was in great shape, but the heat was really getting to her. She was used to running in a gym with air conditioning and built in fans on the treadmill. She didn't fare well in the actual outdoors. She looked to Jake. She envied him at that moment. He was sweating just as much, but he didn't seem at all tired. He loved being outdoors. He was a fan of hiking, biking, and all things outside. He would much rather climb a mountain than use a stair climber at All About Fitness.

They finally reached their destination. They had gone up the long driveway to the farmhouse. They'd passed the horse coming in, but they didn't stop to let Amy visit. Jake looked around. He saw an old truck parked by the barn.

"See," he said, "they might be home."

"Good," Amy said.

As they reached the front steps of the home, they noticed the entire front porch was decorated with hanging flypaper. There were strips by the dozens, hung from the porch roof, hung from the awning, hung from the columns, even hung around the tree next to the house. Amy swatted a fly from her arm.

"Guess they hate flies as much as I do," she said to her boyfriend. He was busy visually inspecting the house.

"Yeah," he replied, "guess so."

He noticed the house appeared to be in decent condition, minus the peeling paint and the not so neatly hung arsenic wallpaper strips.

They reached the door. The main door to the home was open, and a screen door was the only thing keeping the home secure. Jake searched each side of the doorway for a doorbell but found none. He knocked lightly on the wood paneling to the side of the screen door. No one responded.

"Hello," Jake said loudly. "Anyone home?" He knocked again.

"Maybe no one's here," Amy suggested.

"The door's open. Of course they're here."

"Can I help you kids with something?" A booming voice came from behind them.

Startled, the couple whirled around with a jump. They let out a sigh of relief when they saw Jameson, a sweet older gentleman, standing there in his overalls.

"Hi there, sir," Jake started. "My name is Jake, and this is my girlfriend, Amy."

"Hello," she said when Jake pointed to her.

"We have gotten ourselves into kind of a bind," Jake went on. "You see, our car is just up the road, and we have a flat tire. Our phones have no service whatsoever out here, and we were really hoping that you might be so kind as to let us use your phone to see about getting a tow into town or maybe someone to come out with a spare. If it's not a trouble of course."

"Oh," Jameson said as he tossed the thought around his head. "Well, sure. That would be no trouble at all. Here, come on in. Get out of this sun. I'll call Hal at the shop for you." He moved past them and opened the screen door for them to enter.

"Thank you so much, sir. We really appreciate it," Jake said.

"Jameson Briggs." Jameson motioned for Amy and Jake to enter the house.

"Thank you, Mr. Briggs," Amy said.

They walked into the home and were instantly hit with the slight hint of a very foul yet unmistakable odor. The couple winced at the smell out of sheer instinct.

"Oh," Jameson said, noticing their reaction, "yeah. Sorry about the smell. I'm pretty sure a damned possum crawled under the house and found its end down there. I haven't been able to fetch him on out. The smell you get used to; it's the damned flies I can't stand."

"Hence all the flypaper," Jake said, attempting conversation.

"Huh? Oh, right. Yes. I hang that stuff everywhere," Jameson said. "The Misses, well, she hates them flies, too." Jameson showed them into the living room, where Jake and Amy took a seat on the sofa. "I'll just make a quick call over to Hal and see if he can get out here. Make yourselves at home."

"Thank you," they said, almost in unison.

Mr. Briggs made his way into the kitchen as the two sat silently on the sofa. The pair was disappointed to find little relief from the heat indoors. It was almost as hot inside as it was out. Amy looked around the room at all the figurines. There were several porcelain cats, placed in no particular order, all around the room. There were cats on the end tables, cats over the fireplace; cats, cats, cats.

Jameson appeared back in the room.

"You have a lovely collection of cats here," Amy complimented.

"Huh?" Jameson said. "Oh, right. The cats. Those are Amelia's. She loves cats. 'Never had any real ones though. She's allergic."

"Oh, I'm sorry," Amy said.

"It's alright. We don't need any cats around here anyway. Back to the matter at hand. I am sorry to say, Hal is not in today being that it's Sunday and all. I forgot it was Sunday. Nobody's open on Sunday."

"Oh," Jake said, hanging his head. He was really wishing he'd never given his spare to his brother. "Well, thank you so much for your help. We sure appreciate it. Do you know of anywhere we might be able to get a room for the night?"

"Well," Jameson said, "the inn's been closed for over a year now. Fire swallowed her up. The next town over is Hailey, but that's over an hour from here. Why don't you two just stay here tonight? I'll take you to fetch some of your things from your car, and you can just wait here 'til Hal opens up in the morning."

"Gosh, thank you Mr. Briggs, but we wouldn't want to be an imposition..." Jake said.

"No imposition at all," he replied.

"Well," Jake said looking to his girlfriend. She shrugged and so he continued, "if it's okay with Mrs. Briggs."

"Oh, Amelia don't mind. I'm sure she'd love the company. She's napping now, but you can meet her at dinner."

"Oh, gosh," Jake said, "guess we should be quiet then."

"Nah," Jameson said, "she sleeps a lot. She's out like a light. Come on. Let's you and I go get your things."

"Okay, then. You alright here, Aims? We'll be back," he said, turning toward Amy.

"Sure. No problem. I'll go meet the horse." Amy was clearly uncomfortable, but she didn't want to appear to be rude or overly anxious. She wasn't so sure about spending the night in a strange house with people she didn't know, but she knew they didn't really have any other options, except for maybe camping out in the car, and that was something she feared even more. She required the comforts of indoor plumbing and never had enjoyed sleeping while surrounded by trees, strange shadows, and an unknown number of animal eyes peering at her.

The three of them walked back out into the blinding light. The house wasn't air conditioned, but there was at least a ceiling fan in the living room. Amy found the heat outside excruciating.

The men walked to Mr. Briggs' old Chevy, and Amy walked herself down the drive a ways to the corral where the horse was grazing.

"Hey there, pretty boy," Amy cooed at the animal. She made a clicking sound inside her cheek, which gave the horse cause to instantly look up from the grass he was nibbling on and come on over to see what she might have to offer him.

Jameson and Jake rolled up to her in the loud old truck and paused for a moment.

"Now, don't let old Lightning here give you a hard time," Jameson said.

"Okay," Amy said, laughing. "I won't."

The men waved and rolled down the rest of the driveway and out onto the hot, hot highway asphalt.

Amy let the horse smell her hand. He inspected it, expecting to find a treat. When he found she had nothing to give him, he quickly withdrew interest. He let her pet him for a moment, but he then felt compelled to return to his grass.

"Well gee, Lightning," Amy said, "so nice to meet you, too." She laughed as she watched the horse graze.

Inside the Chevy, Jameson and Jake rolled along the highway in the direction of Jake's three wheeled wagon.

"So," Jake said, playing with the air vents. Nothing was coming from them. He quickly deducted that the air in the truck didn't work and gave up. "You sure Amelia won't mind us staying the night?"

"No, she'll be fine with it," Jameson said. "Since the accident, she doesn't really get out, so I'm sure she'll love the company."

"Accident?" Jake asked. He instantly wanted to withdraw the word, but it had already come out. He knew it might be too personal a question to have asked, but it was already on the table. "I'm sorry, I mean..."

"No. It's okay," Jameson said. "About five months back Amelia and I were in the kitchen. It was just after dinner. She had the door to the cellar open. She was about to go downstairs. She turned to tell me something, and that's when..." he paused for a moment and took a deep long breath, "that's when she fell."

"Oh, I'm so sorry," Jake said. "Is she okay?" He knew the answer was likely a negative one, but he felt he had to ask.

"She has her days, but the poor thing can't walk anymore. I have to take care of her. I think it gets her down, but I try to keep her motivated. She's a trooper that one. I love her with everything I've got." Jameson looked out ahead of him and saw the SUV pulled onto the dirt shoulder of the road. He pulled in behind it. "How about that girl of yours? You gonna marry her?"

"Well," Jake said, "yes actually. That is if she'll have me." He laughed a little. "This trip was supposed to be this huge romantic getaway. We're headed to this bed and breakfast in Yorkton, and on the way, we were supposed to stop at the falls, and I was going to do it then. I mean, I'm still going to, just not today I guess. I'm proposing. I had this ring made and everything. She's going to love it. I hope. I'm a nervous wreck."

"Ah," Jameson said, "she'll say yes, son. Don't worry. You'll still get your perfect moment."

"Yeah," Jake said, "I guess so. Just have to make sure I keep this ring hidden from her in the meantime." Jake patted his front shirt pocket.

"The ring's right there in your pocket?"

"Yep. Guess I better find a better place to put it for now." Jake opened the passenger side door and leapt out onto the dirt.

"Probably best," Jameson agreed. "Need help?"

"No, thanks. I'll just grab a couple of our bags and we should be good to go."

At the car, Jake took the satchel he'd put the ring in from his pocket and placed it inside his shaving kit. He knew Amy wouldn't look there. He put the kit back into his overnight bag and zipped it up. He grabbed one of her bags, checked to make sure she had pajamas and a change of clothes inside, knowing if he didn't bring back a necessity he'd be in trouble, and headed back for the truck. He put the bags in the truck bed and clicked his clicker. The horn honked twice and the tail lights flashed.

"Fancy," Jameson said.

"Yeah, well, fancy's no good when you can't go anywhere," Jake joked.

"Guess not."

Jameson turned the truck around on the seemingly abandoned highway and headed toward the farmhouse.

Amy had given up on Lightning and decided to go back into the house. Her thoughts went to the bed and breakfast, and she wondered if she should call to let them know they'd be a day late checking in. She went for her phone again. Taking it from her pocket, she remembered there was no service. She at least had been smart enough to put the number for the place in her phone before they left.

12

Amy paused on the porch, cell phone in hand. She scrolled through her contacts and found the number.

She opened the screen door and tried to shut it slowly so as not to make any noise with the springs. She glanced up the stairs and listened. Nothing. Having just entered the house after being out in the fresh, all be it hot air, she turned her nose up at the stench. Her thoughts went to that poor rotting animal under the house. She wondered what must have happened to it. She continued on into the kitchen where she found a phone hanging on the wall. There was a door right next the phone. It seemed like a pantry door, perhaps an entry to a cellar. It was boarded up. Whatever it was, no one was getting in it. She shrugged and picked up the receiver of the phone, listening for a dial tone. Nothing.

"Hmm," she said, scrunching up her face.

She tried again, playing with the buttons. Nothing. Just then, her thoughts were broken by the roar of the truck wheeling back up the driveway. She hung the phone back up in its cradle and walked out to the porch. Mr. Briggs was right about the odor. She barely even noticed it anymore. It had only been a few minutes, but she was already adjusting.

She watched on as Jake and Mr. Briggs came up the steps with the two bags.

"Think I got everything you need for the night," Jake said proudly as he reached the porch.

"Thanks, babe," Amy said. She gave him a quick peck on the cheek.

"Young love," Jameson cooed. "Nothing like it. I remember those days, but I'll tell ya, it just gets better from here." He smiled at the couple.

They smiled back and Amy gave Jake a hug, though he couldn't hug back with his hands full.

"Alright, let's get in out of the heat," Jameson suggested. The two lovebirds followed him into the house.

Amy laughed a little to herself. *Let's get out of the heat into more heat,* she thought. The house was only maybe a few degrees cooler than it was outside. The upside was of course, there were a lot less flies inside than out.

Jake winced a little at the reintroduction to the foul smell, but he soon got somewhat used to it, too.

"There's a small room here downstairs," Jameson said, motioning for the couple to follow. "You can set up camp here."

The three walked past the staircase down a short hall and turned into a tiny bedroom on the right.

"Bathroom's right across." Jameson pointed back through the door. "Think you'll be okay in here?"

"Of course. It's perfect," Jake said graciously. "You're sure this isn't too much trouble?"

"No, no. It's fine. We don't get many visitors. It will be nice to have someone around, even if just for today." Jameson smiled kindly. "Well I'll leave you two for a minute. I have to get some hay out to Lightning before he starts whinin'."

"Thank you," the couple said in harmony.

Jameson walked out the door, down the hall, and the two heard the springs of the screen door stretch and snap back as the old man left the house.

The pair looked around the room. It was small but brightly lit. There was a large window with a white lace covering.

There was a familiar buzzing noise coming from the entryway. Amy pointed to the ceiling corner by the door. Jake followed her point to find a strip of flypaper there, its latest victim trying desperately to free himself.

"Well, at least they're not on you, right?" Jake said, recognizing her revulsion.

"Yeah, but there sure are a lot of them." Amy sighed.

"I know it's not the romantic weeklong vacation we'd planned." Jake came to his girlfriend's side and put an arm around her waist, drawing her toward him. "But I promise it still can be. Tomorrow we'll get back on our way, and we'll get our perfect trip."

Amy pouted.

"Hey," Jake went on, "look at it this way, it sure will be a fun story for the grandkids. This one time grandma and grandpa got stranded in the middle of nowhere, and these kind strangers..."

"Grandkids, huh?" Amy smiled. She loved when Jake mused about their future.

"You betcha!" He said. "I figure we'll have at least ten of 'em. If our five kids each have two, we'll be set. Our own little tribe."

"Whoa, whoa, buddy. Slow down. Let's maybe plan to get a dog first and see where that goes." She laughed.

"Deal. Come on. Let's go see if Mr. Briggs needs help with anything."

"Hey," Amy stopped Jake as they went toward the door. "You think Mrs. Briggs is alright? It seems like she's been asleep all day."

"Yeah," Jake answered. "Jameson said there was an accident a while back. She's just not her usual self."

"Oh," Amy said, giving Jake's arm a squeeze. "So sad."

Jake kissed his concerned girlfriend on the forehead and led her out to the porch.

They gave Jameson a hand with Lightning, and Amy threw out some scratch for the chickens in the barn. She wondered if this was something she could see herself doing in the future; her and Jake on a farm, caring for horses and

15

chickens and all their five kids; teaching their children the ins and outs of farming, though they really knew nothing of the subject. Then she flashed back to reality. Air conditioning, gym memberships, Starbucks on every corner; these weren't things she could see herself living without. It was a nice thought anyway.

After an hour of shadowing Jameson, the couple agreed to help him prepare for dinner. Jake and Amy set the table for four.

"Why don't you two go enjoy the sunset from outside. I'll get dinner ready." Mr. Briggs handed them each a cold beer from the refrigerator.

"You sure?" Amy asked.

"Sure! Go on. You're our guests. I'll let you know when we're ready."

The pair thanked Jameson and headed for the front porch.

As they walked out the screen door, they were once again greeted by hot summer air. The sun was going down, but the heat was still putting up a fight.

They took a seat on the top porch step.

"Look at all those nasty things," Amy said as she looked around at the lifeless flies gathered on the paper fly strips.

"Isn't that how you like 'em though?"

"Yep. Dead."

Jake put his arm around Amy and kissed her on the forehead.

"I'm sorry this isn't exactly what you had envisioned, but I'll make it up to you. Promise. Tomorrow is a new day."

"Damn right you'll make it up to me," Amy joked. "It's fine. This is fine. I could love you from anywhere."

"Yeah, me too."

They gazed at the sunset and drank down their drinks. Almost an hour had passed before Jameson came to the screen door to let them know dinner was ready.

"Great," Jake said. "I'm starved."

Amy and Jake made their way around the flypaper and back into the house. Their noses were met by the memory of the dead possum below the house. They winced and looked at each other briefly, exchanging half smiles.

"Come on now," Jameson said, "have a seat."

There were three dishes set in the middle. They were having chicken, corn on the cob, and bread.

"Looks fantastic, Mr. Briggs," Amy said.

"Yeah. Thank you so much. You've been so kind," Jake added.

"No need to thank me, kids. We're happy to have you." Jameson smiled. "I have to get Amelia. Go ahead and serve yourselves up. We'll be right down."

They heard Jameson make his way up the creaky stairs. When he reached the top of the steps, there was the sound of a door cracking open. His voice could be heard, but his words couldn't be made out. From what they could hear, his tone was sweet and patient.

Amy looked to her lover and squeezed his hand as it lay on the table. He winked at her and smiled.

"Bread?" Jake offered.

"Let's wait for them, babe."

"Okay." He squeezed her hand back.

They heard the top step creak and footsteps coming down each step that followed. Jameson came around the corner of the doorway, holding his invalid wife in his arms. There was a shawl wrapped around her, face hidden. She seemed so fragile.

Amy looked on in concern. Her heart sank at the site of her. All she could see was her dress and her feet, covered by long socks with booties. She seemed stiff. Amy felt terrible, imagining she was in great pain. She hadn't heard yet the details of the accident, but she knew it must have been horrible.

She threw a saddened look in Jake's direction who returned the look with his own sympathetic half smile.

Jameson placed Amelia in her chair. He lowered the shawl from her face and wrapped it around her shoulders.

Amy let out a horrified gasp at what she saw when the shawl dropped. She sat frozen. Jake leapt from his chair, head swirling. He wasn't sure what he had to do next; what does one do in these kinds of situations?

Jameson kissed his wife on the forehead and scooted her chair in toward the table.

"I'll serve you, dear," he said to her sweetly.

"Jake..." Amy said shakily, not taking her eyes off the old couple.

Jake took a step toward her and put his hand on her shoulder as if to signal they needed to leave.

"Amelia, meet our guests," Jameson said as he put a piece of bread on her plate. "That's Amy, and that nice young man there is Jake."

Amy's eyes were beginning to tear up. She was still frozen, unable to look away.

Jameson smiled and looked to the couple for their response. He seemed disconcerted by their current state.

"Well," Jameson said, "this is my beautiful Amelia."

"Jameson," Jake said awkwardly, "Jameson, she's..."

"I'm sorry. She's shy. We haven't really had any visitors in quite some time. Since the accident, she doesn't like to see people much. Don't worry, she's happy to have you here." Jameson looked proudly at his wife. "Okay, well, go on and dig in. Don't be shy. Fill your plates. Here." He passed the bread bowl.

Amy didn't know what else to do but take it from him. A tear found its way out and moved down her cheek. Her face was so hot, the tear felt like a tiny ice cube as it made a trail.

"Amy," Jake said nervously. Nothing followed.

She put a piece of bread on her plate.

"Jake," Jameson said. "Sit down, son."

"Look," Jake said, "I think we need to go." He grabbed at Amy's shoulder again, shaking it a little this time, trying to make her move. She didn't. She couldn't.

"Go where? Nonsense. Sit down," Jameson said sternly.

Jake looked at Amy. She was still crying silently. Not moving. The bread sat lonely on her plate.

Jake slowly moved back to his seat in disbelief. He sat and stared at the couple across from him.

"Mr. Briggs," Jake said carefully, "Amelia is..." he didn't know what to say next. Could this old man really be overlooking the very obvious fact that his wife was sitting at the dinner table, decaying? How long had she been dead? Why did he not see it? It suddenly became clear to the couple that the flypaper had a very distinct purpose and there likely wasn't an animal under the house.

"Is the most beautiful woman in the world?" Jameson said. "I always thought so." He smiled and grabbed Amelia's hand gently. It made a grotesque cracking sound when he touched it. He seemed aware she was fragile and pulled his hand away. He started putting food on her plate.

"I don't know that she'll need that Mr. Briggs," Jake said, trying to make sense of this. Trying not to upset this disturbed man.

"Yeah," Jameson said sadly, "her appetite hasn't quite been the same since the accident."

"What happened?" Amy asked quietly. As soon as she heard herself say it, she regretted asking.

"I told Jake all about it earlier. She was going into the cellar one afternoon and she fell down the stairs. Poor thing," he said as he turned to her. He looked at her deteriorated face. "Don't look at me like that Amelia," he said to her. Tears began to form in his eyes. "You know it was an accident." He tilted his head to the side. "Don't say that."

Amy turned for the first time to Jake. A look of sheer terror was painted on her face. He motioned toward the door with his eyes. Neither of them actually moved though.

"She still blames me," Jameson said. "It was an accident. I didn't mean for this."

"For what?" Amy asked, again instantly wishing she hadn't. She didn't even know where the words came from. they just appeared and then echoed endlessly and regrettably in her head.

"We were fighting. Something stupid. She had opened the door and was standing at the top of the steps. She was holding these soup cans. I hate soup from a can." Jameson looked to his wife and smiled a little. "She knows I hate soup from a can. I pushed her. I didn't mean to do it. I don't know why I did it. She hurt herself real bad. Those stairs. Those stairs just ruined her. She hasn't forgiven me. I just know it. Forgive me," he said, turning his attention back to Amelia.

"Jake," Amy whispered.

"Look, Jameson..." Jake tried to choose his words very carefully, but he couldn't find any.

"It's okay. Sorry, kids," Jameson said. "Let's eat." He started passing the food to Jake.

Jake took each item and set it down in front of him, putting nothing on his plate.

"Come on, now," Jameson pleaded. "I didn't mean to dampen the mood. I'm sorry. Eat up. We have all this food."

"I don't think we're going to stay," Jake said.

Amy held her breath as she anticipated Jameson's response.

"What do you mean? We're all set here. There's nowhere to go."

"Thank you for your hospitality," Jake continued. "We are grateful, but I think we've imposed enough. We should be on our way."

"On your way? Wait, what's goin' on here?" Jameson was getting angry. "Is our country cookin' not good enough for your delicate city taste? That it?"

"No, no," Jake said, "I'm sorry. That's not what I meant. We just don't want to be in the way here."

"I said you're not, you're not! Amelia was looking forward to this. How dare you come into our home and insult us this way!" Jameson stood from his chair.

"Jake!" Amy shrieked this time.

Jake and Amy got to their feet. Jake grabbed Amy's hand. They started backing toward the doorway.

"Our stuff," Amy said.

Jake's mind flashed to the ring he'd gotten Amy. She would have loved it.

"We'll get new stuff," he whispered.

"You're not going anywhere. Amelia and I won't stand for it." Jameson made his way around the table and approached the pair. Jake's eyes flashed to the cabinet in the corner. There were several guns inside, but the farmer was closer to the cabinet than he was. Jameson noticed Jake's recognition of the guns behind the glass. His face twisted into anger.

"You wouldn't even know what to do with one," Jameson said. He went for the cabinet himself and pulled out a shotgun.

"Run, Amy, run!" Jake yelled.

"No," she said, pulling his arm to get him to go with her.

"Just run!"

She dropped his arm and turned for the door. He hesitated a moment and saw Jameson grab a couple shells for the shotgun he'd selected. His first thought was to get to him and grab it from him, but Jameson was too far, and for an old man, too fast. He was already loaded by the time Jake went through the scenario in his head. He turned and ran out the front door behind Amy. She had a few second head start, but the running suddenly seemed futile and Jake regretted not trying to tackle the farmer as he ran behind her.

The sound of the screen door springing to action came behind them.

Jake heard a shot and watched Amy drop to the ground.

"No!!!!" he yelled out. His mind went back to the house, back to the ring, back to the gun cabinet. If he had stayed and faced the man, Amy would still be running. Jake stopped in his tracks. Head swirling. He heard another shot, then, he heard nothing. No more noise, no more thoughts, no more regrets and indecision; he was gone.

Twenty minutes later, the dinner commenced.

"I'm so sorry, my love," Jameson said as he kissed his bride's boney hand. "But look, they've decided to stay after all. And see there; they're engaged." He pointed to Amy's finger. There was a big shiny ring on it, the one Jake had intended to give her.

Amy and Jake sat in their chairs, full plates in front of them. They stared blankly into the nothing.

"They're going to stay for a while, dear," Jameson said. He waited for a response then continued, "I knew you would like that." Jameson swatted at a fly with his right hand. "Tomorrow, I think I'll work on getting up some more flypaper."

The Apartment

I shot up in bed; my tired eyes forced themselves open. They took a moment to adjust to the dark. I searched the room. Panic began to set in as my brain tried to make sense of the unfamiliar walls and shadows. Then I saw a box come into focus. *SARAH'S BEDROOM* was scribbled on the side in giant, black letters. It was one of the moving boxes I'd so lovingly prepared days before. This was my new room, in my new place; my first apartment, all my own. I realized I had been holding my breath the entire time. I relaxed back onto my pillow and took a deep breath in.

I moved my feet in the bottom of my covers, feeling for my trusty companion, Charlie. She wasn't there. My mind went back to why I had woken to begin with. A crash. Did I hear something in the living room? I tried to remember what stirred me. I then heard something come from the other side of my bedroom door; a loud rustling sound, followed by thrashing.

My feet made their way to the carpet. I stood up and clumsily navigated my way around the boxes toward the door. I was surprised to find the door shut. I could have sworn I'd left it open so Charlie could come and go. I swung the door open and walked slowly toward the light switch on the opposite wall. I flipped on the light, half blinding myself. My ears caught the rustling sound again. I followed the sound to a box in the middle of the room. It had fallen from the chair next to it and was now snuggling the carpet. I moved toward the box and watched it begin to move. It appeared to be under attack from the inside. I could see the side facing up was taped shut. The box had been flipped upside down. I grabbed the sides of the medium sized box marked *BLANKETS,* halting the movement from within. I wasn't careful with the box; I knew it only held two blankets and nothing breakable. I lifted the box with one swift motion and found a very surprised and wide eyed Charlie the cat, wrapped up in a fleece throw. She was giving the blanket a good fight.

"Charlie! Look what you've gotten yourself into!" I said.

She looked up at me and let out a tiny meow.

"That's right," I said to her, "you're busted. Come on."

I picked her up and hauled her toward the light on the opposite side of the room. I used her paw to help me flip the switch.

"Bedtime," I told her. She purred loudly as I toted her to the bedroom.

The next morning, Charlie joined me in the kitchen. I put some canned food on a plate for her and while she chowed down, I went on a hunt for my coffee maker. My parents had given me a brand new coffee machine as a housewarming gift for my first place. It had all the bells and whistles, and most importantly, to them anyway, an auto shut off in case I forgot to turn it off when I left the apartment.

"Bingo!" I found it hiding in the pantry.

I cleaned the decanter, busted open a fresh bag of coffee, and made my first cup of coffee as an independent woman. Somehow, the coffee tasted different. It was the same roast my mom used every day, but it was different making it for myself. Bittersweet. The whole experience was. I was eager to get out on my own and make a life for myself, but I was already missing them and the comforts I had known at home my entire life thus far. They were now two hours away, and I was on my own in a new place, in a new city, with a new job. I still had Charlie though; my trusty sidekick. She'd been there for me the last eight years, and she was my best friend.

We unpacked the stereo, and we got to work. Charlie and I spent the rest of the day tackling the maze of boxes. I somehow had a lot of stuff. I accumulated quite a bit over the years. It was a wonder most of this had fit in my little room back home. A bunch of the new things, dishes, furniture, etcetera, I had been slowly collecting over the last few months in preparation. Some of it, my parents were kind enough to allow garage space for until I could move it, and my couch was delivered the day before. I had been saving for this for over a year, and it had paid off. Looking around, first day down, I had what appeared to be a very put together, adult living space. I was proud.

"We did it, Char," I said, grabbing up my fuzzy buddy. I snuggled up with her on the couch and settled in to watch a movie. It was perfect.

That night, I went to bed with a smile. I set the alarm next to my bed and then set my cell phone alarm as a backup. I couldn't risk not waking up for my first full day at the agency.

I fell fast asleep and was mid fairly awesome dream, when I was startled awake by another crashing sound, just like the one the night prior.

"Charlie! Come on!" I shouted toward the bedroom doorway. I then realized I could feel the weight of my cat on my feet. She was on the bed. So what was in the living room? I waited a moment, and then I heard it again. I sat straight up in bed. Charlie's eyes were trained on the doorway. I ran through a list of things in my head; the front door was locked. I had triple checked it before I went to bed. The sliding glass door in the living room was locked; also triple checked. No one could have gotten in. I heard it again. All the boxes had been unpacked. What was this banging? Three loud noises; something dropped to the floor, but what? Did I leave stuff teetering on the counter or the table? No.

I grabbed a soccer trophy I'd displayed from the desk in my room and gripped it one hand, moving slowly toward the doorway. The door was open this time. I quickly flipped on the bedroom light. As light poured out into the living room, I thought I noticed a shadow take a little longer than the rest to disappear. I blinked my eyes rapidly and shook my head. *Did I really see that? No. No way.* I made my way timidly toward the opposite side of the room and flipped on the living room light. No lingering shadows. No more noise. Stillness; quiet; nothing. Charlie came toward me from the bedroom. She was crouched low and walking very carefully across the carpet. She looked from side to side as if she was scared something would jump out at her.

"It's nothing," I said aloud, trying to reassure both of us. "See."

She straightened upward and calmed. I looked around, trying to discern where that noise had come from. The kitchen area had a bar, where I had two bar stools. They were both on the floor.

"Huh," I said. "Weird." I bent down and propped them back up in their places. I used my hand to test their stability on the plush carpet. Maybe the carpet was too fluffy and uneven to properly support their legs. Odd explanation, but possible. Satisfied enough to let it be for the night, I made my way back to the bedroom. Nestled into my covers, with Charlie relaxed onto my left foot, I replayed what happened in my mind. There were three crashes, weren't there? Three. Two stools; three crashes. Maybe I'd imagined the third. It was nothing. Even so, I was rattled. I had a small TV in the bedroom. I turned it on. I was comforted by the glow of the television. I left it on the rest of the night.

I woke to sunlight peeking in through the blinds. I was reminded that I needed to invest in some curtains. I rolled over and stretched toward the night stand. I glanced at the clock. There were no red numbers glancing back. Adrenaline ran through my veins. I reached for my phone. It was 8:34am. Neither alarm had gone off. I had to be at work at nine.

I leapt from my bed and ran for the bathroom. I did a three minute makeup job and tied my hair back, praying it resembled some sort of trendy *I totally meant to create the just out bed look* look. I threw on my best go-get-em outfit and ran for the door. Just as I went to turn the lock, something caught the corner of my eye. My head turned toward the kitchen. Every cabinet door was wide open.

"What the hell?" I looked down at Charlie. She was staring up at me blankly.

As I rounded the corner of the counter I could see that it wasn't just the doors; the drawers were all pulled open as well. I looked around, not sure what I was looking for exactly. Nothing unusual stood out. Remembering the hurried state I was in, I quickly shut the drawers and the cabinets, and I ran for the door.

I was now left with eight minutes to get to an office that was only six miles away, but in LA traffic, I was actually seventeen minutes from actually getting to my destination. I trotted through the lobby and powered down the hall to the suite where I would embark on my new career as a mail room girl slash errand mule slash, hopefully someday, talent submission assistant for a semi-well known children's talent agent. This was a step up from biscuit babe at the mom and pop restaurant I had worked in the three years prior to my grand journey to Los Angeles. I was headed places; if I still had a job anyway.

Taking a deep breath, I swung open the door of Lauren Landis Talent, and head held high, I prepared for my first bout with trouble in the workplace.

Lauren Landis stood proudly at the front, next to the receptionist. She was reprimanding him for not taking down a phone number correctly.

Shit.

Her eyes, filled with fire, broke away from him and focused on me. She squinted.

My first instinct was to look away; look down; look anywhere but right at her. I felt I might turn to stone if we kept contact. I didn't though. I chose to take my lumps.

"Well," she hissed, "I would like to say that perhaps I was mistaken and I told you to be here at nine thirty, however, it is rare that I make mistakes, and I am sure I told you nine."

The insanely good looking guy behind the desk raised his eyebrows. He was clearly relieved the attention had been drawn away from him, but he looked genuinely concerned for me.

"You did say nine, and I apologize. My alarm didn't go off, and then the traffic was..."

"The traffic?" She squinted harder. "There's always traffic, dear. Please make this your first note, Sig Alert is your new best friend. It tells you exactly what the traffic is like at all times. You get up early and check it every ten minutes to make sure nothing's changed. Got it? In this town early is on time, on time is late, and late...well, late just doesn't happen. Although, being that you are so late, I would think you might

29

have taken a couple extra minutes to do something a little different with that hair."

"Yes, Miss Landis. I am so sorry." My hair. I guess I couldn't pull off the *I meant it to look messy* look. I could feel my face getting warm. I knew I must have been a terrible shade of red. The awareness of this fact only fueled the heat, making my cheeks unbearably hot.

"Save the sorrys, dear. Good lord, you sound like my ex-husband. Sorry; sorry; sorry. Well, don't do it in the first place, and then we'll have nothing to be sorry for, right?" She smiled from the side of her mouth. She appeared almost amused, but her brow never changed positions, completely muddying my read on her. She chuckled to herself, but even so, I was mostly sure she wasn't joking. "Alright. 'Enough of this. Let's get you acclimated. This darling boy you heard me so lovingly teach the importance of not transposing numbers is Finch."

"Hi Finch," I said, placing my hand over the desk.

"It's actually Dustin Finch." He met my hand with his and gripped it. He applied the perfect amount of pressure. Every time I shake someone's hand I am reminded of a lesson my father taught me on the importance of a good handshake. When I met Lauren Landis, a handshake was out of question as she is terrified of germs. It was almost a wonder she made it in the business of marketing children. Children are basically human petree dishes.

"Yes," Lauren said, "his name is Dustin Finch, but I'm having him try Finch on as his first name. I like it better." She side smiled again. I still just couldn't tell if I was supposed to be laughing politely at her humor, or if I was hearing her honestly announce aloud she thought his name sucked.

All the same, I smiled at him and gave a "nice to meet you. My name's Sarah". When our eyes met, I again had the instinct to immediately look away. He was probably the most gorgeous male I had ever seen in person. He had giant brown eyes and a smile that was complimented by perfectly straight teeth and adorable matching dimples in his cheeks.

"Come on now. 'Lots to show you," Lauren said.

I followed closely behind her as she walked me down the hall.

"Let's not spend too much of our time focusing on Mr. Finch back there, okay sweetie? I'm not fond of office drama, and I really wouldn't want you to get in over your head."

I had gathered she was a stern woman, but though I wasn't entirely sure of the implication's meaning, I knew enough to feel insulted.

"Well, I..."

"Oh don't get me wrong, dear. You're lovely. I just mean, I don't want you to lose focus."

"I won't," I assured her. "Focus is my middle name." I smiled.

"Huh," she said, squinting again.

Around 5:30, I was released from first day hell and back on the dreaded highway. I didn't know the streets well enough to avoid the highway yet, but judging from the traffic just getting to the on ramp, it might not have made much difference.

Stopped in the fast lane, which at the moment seemed like the slowest of all the lanes, I decided to call my mom to tell her all about my miserable day. I told her about Lauren and her contempt for humans. I told her about the beautiful Dustin Finch. When I was done venting and relaying, she asked about the apartment.

"Oh, yeah. Weirdest thing," I said. "This morning all the cabinets in the kitchen were wide open."

"Hmmm," my mother replied, "maybe you have a mouse."

"A mouse? Gross! Mice open doors?"

"Sure they can, from the inside. Shockingly strong, rodents." She laughed.

"And drawers? The drawers were open, too."

"I don't know about that, but it is probably just a little Mickey. You might want to set a trap or two. You don't want him getting into your food boxes or pooping on your plates."

"That's disgusting."

"Yeah, well, it's what they do," she said.

"I wonder why Charlie hasn't found him."

"Are you kidding? That fat cat is too lazy to go on a mouse hunt." She laughed again.

"Well I'm glad you think this is so funny. Alright, well I am almost to my exit, and I am starving. So I'm going to get home and get dinner started."

"Ok, love you. Watch for mouse poop."

"Ha! Thanks. Love you, too."

When I got home, I was pleased to find the cabinets and drawers all firmly closed. Charlie couldn't wait to tell me all about her day. She meowed me into the kitchen, and I plopped some wet cat food onto a plate for her.

I triple checked the box of brown rice before I got started. While my dinner was cooking, I pulled things out of the cupboards at random and closely inspected them. No evidence of tampering by rodents. I was glad for that, but I felt oddly uneasy at the same time. Would I have really felt better if I had found proof that there was a plague carrying invader in my home? Maybe not, but I felt it left the kitchen phenomenon unexplained.

Putting it out of my mind, I continued with my evening and found myself snuggled into bed once again. I fell asleep to the glow of the TV.

I woke a few hours later to an unsettling feeling. My eyes darted from side to side. The television was still on. I could hear the audience laughter of a syndicated sitcom. This was calming. I then tried to move my foot to check for Charlie. My foot didn't move. I tried to lift my head to look down, but my head wouldn't move. My arms, my hands, my legs, my feet; I couldn't move any part of my body except for my eyes. They moved rapidly, searching my limited range of vision. Panic took over. I tried to scream, but my voice was only present inside my head. No sound would come from my lips. I couldn't move my mouth. My vocal chords were frozen. Nothing. I was breathing so hard I almost drowned on oxygen. I felt myself getting light headed.

Then I saw it. From the corner of my eye, I saw a shadow. Something in the corner, near the ceiling. The light from the television flickered and changed the other shadows on the walls, morphing them into different shapes and streaks, but this one did not change with the others. This one stayed. I wanted desperately to turn my head toward it, to see it better, but I could not.

I held my breath. I gave up trying to scream. I thought maybe if I stayed even stiller than I already was, maybe it would move along; it wouldn't see me, whatever *it* was.

This is insane, I thought. *Move! Move!* I tried to will my body to do something, anything.

And then the shadow began to move. It slid slowly downward. I thought I could almost hear it sliding down the newly painted wall. *Shadows don't make sounds.*

I couldn't see it anymore. It was out of my line of site. The panic grew stronger. I felt a weight to the left of me on the side of the bed as if someone was pressing down on the mattress. I couldn't see anything next to me; just the flickering colors being cast by the television, and the corner of my nightstand. The pressure on that side of the mattress built, and I felt my body tipping to the left. I still wasn't breathing. I couldn't move. I couldn't breathe. I just knew whatever was there was going to end me.

I didn't want to, but I closed my eyes tight, wishing it away. I screamed in my head for it to stop. I felt the sheets on my bed start to pull away from my chest. My eyes flipped open, and I screamed as loud as I could. I screamed. There was actual sound. My head turned to the left. Nothing. I could move. I could speak. My legs joined my chest as I curled upright against the wall. It was the tightest ball I'd ever twisted myself into. Sweat was pouring from my face. My pajamas and the sheets were soaked with perspiration. My heart was pounding so hard I felt like I might throw up. I was breathing, but not well. I looked all around the room; Left to right; Up and down; Nothing. The same sitcom was still playing out on the television. The audience laughed again as one of the characters cracked a joke. Everything in the room was exactly as it had been just a moment before, except it was gone. There was no lurking shadow; no invisible man at my bedside.

Had I dreamed up the whole thing? It was so vivid; so real. Everything in the room was exactly as it was in the nightmare. Every last detail was the same, even the TV show. How was this possible?

Charlie. Where is Charlie?

I didn't see her at the end of the bed. She wasn't nearby. I found my voice again and called to her quietly. Still shaken, I was afraid to announce myself too loudly.

She appeared in the doorway, looking unfazed. She padded across the carpet and leapt up onto the bed. She head butted me a few times and then took her spot at the edge of my comforter.

"Guess it was just a dream, Charlie," I said, trying to calm myself.

I laid awake the next few hours, watching reruns, afraid to fall back asleep. I must have given into it eventually because the next thing I knew, I was being sprung back to reality by the sound of my alarm clock.

My bedroom looked so cozy and inviting in the warm daylight. My cat slept soundly through the beeping. Everything seemed so perfect and serene. What was I afraid of?

I headed to the bathroom. My hand went into the bathroom first so I could turn the light on before my body entered. I was still a little darkness shy. There weren't any windows in the bathroom, so the only light provided was artificial. I tried not to think about my nightmare while I showered.

I attempted singing a little bit, but I couldn't help being a little jumpy still.

Though I still felt like a fish out of water, being at work that day provided a lot of comfort. There were people there, more than adequate lighting, and plenty of distraction. By lunchtime I was in full on zombie mode. I was so tired. I was mindlessly stamping envelopes with a return address and completely zoning out.

"You might want to slow down there, Speedy." Finch's voice came from behind me. I turned to see him coming toward me. "You're going to make the rest of us look bad."

I smiled. "Yeah, well, Lauren wants two hundred of these done by this afternoon so that we can be extra prepared for the week's mailings or something like that."

"You look totally zonked."

"Zonked?" I'd never heard that before, but I was pretty sure it meant I looked like shit. "I didn't exactly get a whole lot of sleep last night."

"Come on." He motioned for me to follow him. "Let's get you some coffee."

"I don't know. I still have all of these..."

"You still get a lunch break. Come on. It's the law." His dimples were showing again. I couldn't say no.

We sat at a small table on the patio of the coffee shop on the corner. People dressed in skinny jeans and scarves tied in different types of knots surrounded us.

"I had no idea there were so many ways to wear a scarf," I said playfully.

"It's the cool uncool thing to do right now I guess," Finch said.

"Like going by your last name?"

"Exactly."

We laughed and drank from the tops of our plastic lids. We settled into shockingly comfortable conversation. I had a tendency to be shy, but with him, I could go on and on about anything. It was like we were old friends.

On our way back to the office, his hand accidentally brushed mine, sending chills up my arm and filling me with flutters.

"Oops," he commented, "getting ahead of myself there."

I giggled nervously. My shyness was creeping back in.

"So, I know I might be out of my league here, but would you like to have dinner with me tonight?"

Was he serious? Out of his league? Wow. I could feel my face heating up again.

"I think I might be able to tear myself away from my busy schedule. Sure."

"Great." He seemed nervous too. This was oddly comforting. "Text me your address. I'll come by around seven."

The rest of my day was spent making phone calls and stuffing envelopes.

When I arrived home, Charlie was waiting to greet me at the door.

"Well hello. What did you do today?"

Charlie let out a long yowl.

"Wow, Char. You had quite a day." I replied. I led her to the kitchen and shook some treats out onto the floor.

I went to my bedroom and quickly turned my attention to the closet. I had a date, and I had no idea what to wear. I tried on seven combinations of shirts, skirts, jeans, and slacks. I finally settled on the very first thing I tried on. Go figure. I spent about an hour fixing my hair and doing my makeup, something I typically didn't put all that much time into, but Finch was really cute. I wanted to make a great first date impression.

Mostly pleased with the final result, I left the bathroom and went to sit on the couch. I flipped nervously through the channels on the TV, constantly checking the time on my phone. There were three light raps at the door. I jumped up and went toward the doorway. I shook out my hands, and took a deep breath. My right eye met with the peephole to find no one. I could see across the hallway to my neighbor's door. The hall was dimly lit as usual. I turned the lock and opened the door, poking my head out. No one.

I shut the door and returned the lock to its defensive position.

"Must be nerves, eh Charlie?" I said to my chubby cat.

I returned to my couch and picked up my phone. *6:54. 'Getting close.* I took up the remote again, and just as I switched to the next channel, something caught the corner of my eye. My head turned left, toward the kitchen. The cabinets were wide open, again. I looked at Charlie. She was busy bathing herself on the carpet.

I got up and walked slowly toward the kitchen. I was on high alert, expecting a giant mutant rodent to jump out at any second. I listened intently, hearing nothing. I waited for any sign of movement. None came. I went to each cupboard, inspecting their insides. Nothing.

A new knock came from the doorway. This one was much louder. I quickly shut all the cabinets and trotted back to the door.

This time, staring back through the peephole, I saw Finch. He was half smiling. *Ugh! Those dimples!*

My hand turned the lock to the left and went for the door knob. I took one more deep breath, and the door was open.

"For you," he said, handing a small bunch of flowers to me.

"Thank you." I knew I was blushing, but this time, I didn't really mind.

"You look incredible," he complimented.

"Thank you, again. So do you."

I motioned for him to come in. I went back to the invisible rodent infested kitchen, and I found the only vase I owned. I took care to unwrap the bundle and cut the ends of the stems under running water before placing them into the glass container. They were perfect. I displayed them proudly on the countertop.

"There."

"They look perfect," he said.

"They are. Thank you. So..."

"Ready? I made a reservation at Padri. Have you been?" he asked.

"No. I haven't. Where's that?"

"It's in Agoura Hills. Best Italian in town. Or out of town, I guess. I thought you would dig the atmosphere."

"Sounds great."

"Great," he echoed. "Let's go."

The restaurant was dimly lit and very romantic. We sat in a corner table away from a lot of the conversation of other patrons. We talked and talked without awkward pauses or lingering silence. It was so comfortable. Even though we chatted about our life stories, it was almost as if we'd known each other forever. Before I knew it, we were getting our doggie bags and walking back to the car. He held my hand in the parking lot and opened the passenger door for me. I expected him to go in for a kiss, but he didn't.

Back in my hallway, he gave me a hug.

"I had a great time," he said.

"Me too." I paused a moment, thinking how to approach my next move without seeming like I was asking for more than I wanted to put out. Finally I just said, "Would you like to hang out for a while? Watch a movie?"

His face lit up.

"Just a movie, I mean." I felt I had to emphasize that I wasn't that kind of girl.

"Sure. Sounds fun," he said, laughing. "And just so you know, I'm not that kind of guy. Just a movie is just right."

"Okay," I blushed. I was embarrassed that I thought I had to clarify to begin with.

We went inside, and I asked him to choose a DVD from my ridiculously huge collection. I'd been obsessed with 80s films and horror movies since I could remember. He decided on a super campy 80s horror film, and my heart fluttered. I'd never met anyone who shared my taste for cheesy monster flicks.

He held my hand on the couch, but he was careful not to sit too close. He was being a perfect gentleman, but about halfway through the movie, I couldn't stand it any longer. I leaned over and kissed him. It was kind of perfect. He had a gorgeous face, manors, great taste in bad movies, and he was a great kisser. What was wrong with this guy that I hadn't seen yet? Then it happened. He pulled my hair. Weird. Such a gentleman all night, and then this? I didn't really appreciate the aggressive move. It was especially odd, because it didn't really match up with what we were doing.

"Hey," I said. "Play nice." I was trying to be cute, hoping he'd get the message.

"What? I thought I was," he pulled away, confused.

"My hair. I haven't really had my hair pulled since my days on the playground."

"Whoa, I didn't pull your hair." He backed away a little further.

"Oh, ok." I winked at him. I was still trying to be playful yet send a clear message at the same time; why girls do that, I don't even know. I should have just said *Hey buddy! I said nothing was gonna happen here, and I meant it!* But instead, I wanted to appear desirable, yet classy.

Still looking confused, he stood up. "Bathroom?" he asked, even though the place was tiny and there was really only one direction to go.

"Right there." I pointed toward the opposite wall.

He left the couch, and I sat there alone, thinking over what had just happened. Just then, I felt a firm yank on my hair again. I felt fingers, wrapped in my tresses and a hard tug. No mistaking it. My breath stopped immediately. I very slowly, very carefully turned my head in the direction of the bathroom, the door was shut; I could see the light come through the bottom off the door. I heard the sink running. I turned my attention very slowly toward the kitchen area, Charlie was sitting on the floor, staring at me, eyes wide. No, I realized, she wasn't staring at me, she was staring past me; almost through me. I was frozen. My hair was released from the grip it was in. I jumped up and turned toward the couch in one swift movement. Nothing. I saw nothing.

Charlie's hackles were up. Her eyes were still fixed on the couch. I heard the bathroom door open behind me. The hissing sound of the filling toilet tank spilled into the room.

"What's up?" Finch's voice broke in over the other sounds.

"There's someone in here," I whispered.

"What? Where?" He was looking around.

"There. Behind the couch." I held my finger up in that direction.

Finch moved quickly toward the couch. He looked behind it, beside it, under it; he even picked up the decorative pillows and looked in the areas they left naked. He was very thorough.

"I don't see anybody," he said. "Did you see somebody?"

"No, I just..." what did I just? None of this made any kind of sense, and if it made all of zero sense to me, how could I possibly explain it to someone else? "I guess I just sort of let my imagination get the best of me."

"Ah, Boogeyman! Well, we are watching a scary movie. Maybe that's it. Or... maybe you have a ghost!" he said, eyes wide. He was laughing. It made me laugh a little. "I bet it was Ghosty who pulled your hair," he joked. If only I could tell him what happened while he was in the bathroom.

"Nah," I said, feigning calm. "I think it snagged on my necklace. Sorry about that."

"No problem. I told you, I'm not that kind of guy." He was so cute. He kissed me on the cheek. "Let's just watch the movie." He grabbed my hand and led me back to the couch. He didn't try to kiss me again. When the movie ended, I felt better having had some time in between me and the last incident.

"I should get going," Finch volunteered. "It's late."

41

"Okay." I stood with him and walked him to the door. "Well thank you. I had a lot of fun. Sorry about the weird..."

"No problem," he said. He kissed me on the cheek again and gave me a hug. "I'll see you in the morning."

"Yep. In the morning," I echoed.

He walked out the door, and I locked it behind him. I rested my body against the wood frame and exhaled. I looked around my little apartment. I grabbed my necklace. Could what I said have been true? Maybe my hair did get wrapped up in the chain. It was possible. It really was the only sane explanation. And who knows about Charlie. Maybe she was just reacting to a bug on the wall. I really was making a whole lot out of nothing.

I brushed it off and headed for bed. That night I fell asleep once again to the glow of the television, with my best friend asleep at my feet. I woke around 3am to an almost stifling heat. The room was incredibly hot. Sweat was pouring from my face. I looked down at Charlie. Her hacks were up again, and she was backing slowly from the edge of the bed. She started hissing at something she could see on the floor. Her head shot up so she could watch the ceiling. She backed further and further. Her behavior made me pull my feet in. She then shot to the head of the bed near me. I sat up in bed, bringing my knees to my chin. She hissed at the same spot on the ceiling. Just then her eye line dropped as I felt a large weight drop onto my bed where Charlie was before this happened. It hit the bed forcefully, and I could feel it move the entire mattress. I stared at the invisible assailant. I saw nothing, but I knew something was there. Charlie knew it too. I saw the left bottom edge of the bed tip. I felt the mattress move in that direction as if something rolled off the corner of the bed. Charlie jumped down and went after it.

"Charlie, no!" I yelled. I didn't know what she was chasing, but I knew she shouldn't be.

I heard her growling near the bed. I carefully peered over the side. She was batting her paw at something. She then chased it out of the room. I heard hissing. My instinct was to get up and get my cat, but fear left me there in bed. I waited; listening. The hissing stopped.

"Charlie?" I called quietly.

I stared at the dark space where the door was cracked open. The light shifted with the television. Shadows danced against the walls. The door moved slightly, forcing me to jump back more firmly against the headboard. It was Charlie. I sighed in relief. She jumped up on the bed and took her spot as if nothing happened.

I reached over and patted her on the head.

"Thanks, buddy," I said, still unsure what had just took place. I knew what I saw, and I also knew there was something I didn't see. But what? The room cooled back to a bearable temperature almost immediately.

I rested back onto my pillow and stretched my feet out slowly. I was hesitant, but I figured it was safe now that Charlie was back at the foot of the bed. After about an hour of watching reruns, I finally fell asleep. I didn't dream at all the rest of the night.

I woke feeling completely out of it. The morning found me exhausted. I sleepily made my way to the bathroom.

I flipped on the lights and the fan and started the shower. All I could think of was how my Mr. Coffee was soon to become my best friend. I stood still in the shower, letting the water run down my body. It felt good. I felt connected to the water. I closed my eyes and let the warmth engulf me. I opened my eyes to find darkness.

Panic fell over me. I felt my eyes trying to adjust. I hadn't gone blind; the lights were off. I listened; the fan had stopped as well. Was the electricity out? I pushed back the shower curtain. There was a tiny strip of light at the bottom of the door. Having no windows in this bathroom quickly became a huge issue. I could feel the panic growing. I was breathing hard; the steam from the shower now felt suffocating. I felt for the knob and turned the shower off as quickly as I could. I reached for the towel rack and felt around for the terry cloth material. I found it. Just as I went to yank it from the rack, I felt a hand on mine; a cold palm and fingers, touching the back of my left hand. I screamed and leapt back to the shower wall. It felt wet and grimy against my skin. I was clutching the towel tightly to me. The lights flipped on. I forced my eyes to readjust. Nothing. I saw the sink. I saw the toilet. I saw the tiles on the floor and the cute bathroom rug I'd picked out just the week before; but nothing else. I jumped out of the shower, and wrapping the towel around me very sloppily I rushed out the door into the safe light of my living room. I was completely shaken from my zombie like daze.

I went to a bar stool and sat, trying to breathe. I looked around. Everything looked so nice and put together. I had really done a great job decorating the place. I laughed. *What an idiot,* I thought. What was I freaking myself out for? Was I really just this scared to live alone? I was clearly making stuff up in my mind. Was I trying to justify a return home perhaps? I hadn't had the actual thought before, but maybe this was my subconscious way of trying to give up and go home to Mom and Dad. I was a grown up, damn it! I could handle this.

I went to the kitchen and poured some coffee grounds into a filter. I filled the side of my Mr. Coffee with water and flipped it on. I propped myself up against the counter and let the familiar smell of brewing coffee waft over me. I was back to reality. I looked around again. I was home. I decided everything was all in my mind, and today was a new day. Today was the day I would grow up and learn to enjoy being an independent woman. Charlie could chase shadows all she wanted, but I was just fine.

Charlie brushed against my legs and made a plea for breakfast. I dished out some canned food onto her kitty plate and watched her eat. She was fine; I was fine; this was fine.

I finished getting ready without incident. When I went back into the bathroom, I played with the light switch. Perhaps I hadn't flipped it all the way on, and it just teetered the other way. It was working fine now.

The rest of the morning went along normally. I got to work to find a smiling Finch sitting at the front desk. His dimples were in full effect.

"Morning Sarah," he greeted me.

"Morning, Finch." I nodded in his direction.

"So, how late did Mr. Ghosty stay last night?" he asked playfully.

"Oh, he left when you did. I guess he's not really a partier," I joked.

"Hmmm, good to know." He winked. "You better get back there. Lauren's having a day..."

"Thanks for the warning."

I walked back to find Lauren in her office scowling at headshots.

"Look at this crap!" she said, tossing an 8x10 across the desk toward me.

"Oh wow," I said, holding up a photo of what appeared to be a thirty year old child.

"When I say natural, young, fun, what do you hear?"

I didn't answer. I knew it was rhetorical.

"I mean really!" she went on. "Could this hack of a photographer be more of an asshole? This child looks like a prostitute! What the hell were they thinking? I can't believe her mother paid for these. He's over. We're putting him on the Don't List. Make sure that gets out in an email to all of our clients. Today."

"'Will do." I placed the awful photo back on her desk and turned to leave.

"Thank you," she said.

I smiled and turned around.

"You're welcome," I returned. This was the first thank you I'd heard from her. Granted, it had only been a few days, but I was certain that Lauren Landis didn't do gratitude.

I walked out the doors and heard her clear her throat, which I had already learned to take as a cue to come back.

"By the way," she said as I peeked in, "your hair is much better like that."

I smiled at her and nodded. I was positive Lauren Landis didn't do compliments either. Today was going great. I couldn't believe it. Maybe it was my new outlook. Maybe my new found can-do attitude made me stand a little taller. Couldn't be sure, but I felt great.

I went through my day with a smile. I was happy to do anything and everything that came my way. Stuffing envelopes was actually fun. Finch and I went to coffee again and had a great conversation about music. He told me about this local dive bar that had an all-ages night twice a month. He wanted to take me to the next one in a couple weeks. Of course I agreed. I had to get a second chance to prove I wasn't insane.

On the way home from work, I called my mom to tell her all about my new crush and what a great time we had on our date. I told her a little about my insanity and the creepy experiences I'd been having around the apartment, but that I was proud to have come to the realization that I was just nervous about being on my own. She agreed but told me I should still set traps around. Charlie was probably chasing the rodent that had made a playground of my kitchen.

It felt nice to talk to my mom. She always made me feel better. I guess I really just needed to talk out my feelings about the move, all the changes in my life, my nerves and apprehensions. It was helpful. After the awesome day I had at work, the invite for a second date, and the great convo with my mom, I was feeling especially good.

At home, I found a happy Charlie, waiting to tell me all about her day. She followed me around, meowing and purring up a storm. I sat on the couch with her for a while and watched a show. She purred happily and fell asleep in my lap. I must have fallen asleep too because next thing I knew I was opening my heavy eyes and scrambling to get to my phone. The ring tone seemed especially loud, but that was probably amplified by the fact I was dead asleep when it went off. The screen showed "Finch Calling". I swiped my finger across the screen to answer.

"Hi," I said, attempting to sound super awake.

"Hey, what are you up to tonight?" he asked.

"Uh," I searched my brain for something cool to say, but I had nothing. "That depends," I said, "what are you up to?" Lame.

"Well, I don't really want to wait 'til the next all-ages show to hang out with you. So I was wondering if you might want to go to a movie with me tonight."

"I guess I could do that." Double lame.

"Alright... well, how about I come by in an hour or so, and we'll pick something out then.

"Sure. See you then," I said. Less lame, but still not my best.

We hung up and I palmed my forehead with my right hand.

"Char, when a boy calls, don't try to be aloof. It doesn't work," I said to my cat.

She blinked at me and rolled over for a belly scratch.

"Exactly," I said.

I put on some music and danced around, getting ready in between my dance moves for another night out with the sexy guy from the front desk. It had occurred to me a few times that Lauren's warning about dating co-workers might be something to take more seriously, but he was just so perfect. So far anyway. Besides, I could handle it right?

I was in the bathroom putting the final touches on my mascara when the knock at the door came. I quickly pushed my makeup into the drawer and wiped down the counter. I trotted toward the door and went for the knob. As I ran over to the door something seemed off. I stepped a few steps backward and looked toward the kitchen. Every single door was open again, including the drawers.

"What the hell?" I put the words into the air.

My attention was turned by a second knock at the door. I went for the knob and swung the door open.

"Hi. Come on in," I said, motioning for Finch to step inside. "Sorry about the kitchen," I continued as he walked through the doorway. "I think I have a mouse, or..." As we got to the kitchen area, I saw all the cabinets and drawers were closed.

"Or..." Finch said.

"Or something." I was confused. I knew what I saw. "Sometimes the cabinet doors open themselves," I admitted. "It might be a mouse or something. Right? They do that?"

"Open doors? Maybe. They're strong little guys," he said smiling.

"But I guess they wouldn't close them would they?" I glared at the kitchen.

"Not unless they were super polite house guest mice." He bent down and pet Charlie. She purred and rolled over for a belly pat. He obliged. She really liked him. I did too.

"So, movies. What's playing?" I asked. "I haven't even looked."

"Well, are you in the mood for funny?"

"Sure!" I said. We decided on a movie and set off for the theater.

As we stepped into the hallway, the lights flickered. I locked the door behind us. As we stepped by each light fixture, a surge happened.

"Man," Finch said, "this place needs an electrician stat. Creepy." He grabbed my hand.

"Yeah," I said. "Creepy." I squeezed his hand and tried to put it out of my mind. It was all purely coincidental. Everything was fine now.

The movie was hilarious. Afterward, my face was twitching from laughing non-stop for an hour and forty-two minutes. We went for an ice cream and took a walk around the Burbank Town Center. I had never been there before. I was amazed by how alive it was. There were twinkling lights, and music, and people everywhere; some of the people were coupled up; some were in groups; some were alone. There were scores of people, moving in different directions; so many faces; an array of voices and sounds of laughter filling the night air. I just sat and soaked it in.

"You act like you've never seen people before," Finch said as he tucked a piece of hair behind my ear for me.

"No, it's just so incredible. You know? So many people all in one place, all with a different destination; a unique agenda. It's just kind of cool, you know?"

"Yeah," he said, "I guess it is. Never really thought of it like that. I mostly just see all this and think, *ugh! What a crowded mess! Look at the rats run.*"

"Ah," I responded, "with an attitude like that, you're going to miss out on the beauty of the world."

"Nope. I have plenty right next to me."

I smacked him playfully. "Come on," I said, tugging his shirt. "Let's get back and see what Mighty Mouse has done to my kitchen."

Charlie was asleep on the couch when we got back to my place. I went to the kitchen. None of the cabinetry seemed ajar. All seemed to be just how we left it.

Finch took a seat next to the sleepy kitty. She head butted his arm and purred loudly. He looked right at home hanging out with Charlie. I sort of liked the way he accented the couch. I know people aren't like throw pillows, but it was kind of a fun thought.

"So," Finch said, "thanks for hanging out again. It was fun. I should probably get." He stood.

"You don't have to take off right this second," I said.

"Well, it's late, and to be perfectly honest with you, I'm nothing without my sleep, so..." he laughed. "In all seriousness, I promised my roommate I would hit up the canyon with him at like 5am, and I haven't hiked in a couple weeks, so I sort of need to get to bed, or else he's going to make me look like a jackass."

"Oh. Gotcha." I went in for a hug, and he touched my face gently with his palm, guiding my mouth toward his. We kissed for what felt like a blissful eternity, but what I knew was only about ten seconds.

"Night." He was blushing.

"Night." I was smiling like an idiot. And he was gone again. I flipped the bolt to the right and leaned my back against the door. I squealed a giddy squeal to myself and trotted over to my buddy.

"I really like him, Char," I said as I scratched beneath her chin. With her face stretching up toward the ceiling in delight and her whiskers forward, she appeared to be smiling. "Exactly," I said. "Come on, buddy. Bed time."

I went into the bathroom, still in a love sick daze. I swung open the mirrored door on the medicine cabinet and retrieved my toothbrush. I hummed as I brushed my teeth, swaying to my own tune. I leaned over and took some water into my mouth from the spout and swished it around. I stood up from the basin and looked at my reflection, but I wasn't the only one in it. I quickly turned around to see no one. I turned back to the mirror to find just me staring back. My heart was racing. What had I really seen? Not a person exactly... a shadow. There was a misplaced shadow, a person shaped shadow, looming behind me. Wasn't there?

I crept slowly back into the living room, making each step as light as I could. I was suddenly very aware of how the carpet felt beneath my bare feet. I saw Charlie, sitting on the floor, happy as ever. She meowed at me and turned toward the kitchen. She was asking for a treat in true Charlie fashion.

I let out a long exhale. I was doing it again. I was letting myself sabotage a perfectly good evening. I shook it off and grabbed the open can of food from the fridge to give Charlie a little heap of pre-bedtime grub.

I made my way to bed, making sure to turn on the television before I flipped off the lights. I snuggled into my sheets and replayed my date in my head. It was such a great night. He was such a great guy. It was the perfect end to a perfect day. I fell asleep smiling.

I woke again to a stifling heat. I could feel beads of sweat running from my forehead, over to my temples, and down my jawline as if following a river trail. I went to wipe the trail away with my left hand, but my hand never came to my face. I tried to move my right hand, nothing. Adrenaline rushed through my entire body. I could feel my hands, but I couldn't move them. I couldn't move my arms, my legs, my feet, or any other part. Once again, I could only move my eyes. My eyes moved around in a panic, searching for reason; searching for a way out; searching for ensured safety. I didn't see any shadows. There wasn't anything unusual in my line of vision. I watched the colored lights bounce off the wall next to me. The TV was still on. But wait, I couldn't hear it. I couldn't hear anything. I couldn't even hear my rapidly beating heart. Silence. Pure silence. Then I saw it, the light shifted on the wall and a new shadow emerged. As the colors flashed and flickered, the dark shadow moved, but it didn't change shape. It slid down from the top of the wall to the floor, out of my range of sight.

Charlie. Where is Charlie? I couldn't look down to see if she was there. I couldn't move my foot to check for her near me. I was stuck. My pulse was racing so fast, my chest ached. I was breathing rapidly, almost choking on the thick air.

Then there was something on me. I felt a pressure on my chest and shoulders. It felt like I was being held down by something very heavy. The sheer weight of it forced my breathing to slow. The pressure rolled to one side, as if it had let up on my right side and was leaning on the left. I couldn't see it. I couldn't make out what it was. I felt it slide toward my left and to the side of the bed. Then hands gripped my left arm. All of my muscles tightened in protest. I couldn't move my limbs, but I felt my muscles grow tight. It felt like I had simultaneous charley horses all around my body. There were three large hands on my left arm, starting at my wrist and working up. Then there were two more hands, cold hands, on my left ankle and shin. And then came the worst. I felt an even larger hand grab onto my rib cage like a scoop. I felt a deep seething agony as it tugged at my ribs. I felt it trying to dig into my stomach through my flesh. All the hands pulled at once, edging me toward the side of the bed. They pulled roughly but slowly. It seemed as if it was taking hours for them to make their large and painful moves. I felt my arm pulled down over the side. I knew I was screaming, but I couldn't hear it. I could feel the burning and tearing in my throat as I screamed for my life, but no sound came to me. My body was pulled over the edge to the ground. I felt every bone shake as I hit the ground with force. The pain in my ribs momentarily subsided as the hands changes their grips. They were now moving to my right side. They were pulling me under the bed. My eyes moved around, back and forth, up and down. I could see every detail of the room, exactly as I'd left it at bed time. My head was pulled up for a split second by my hair, and my eyes caught a glimpse of a popular sitcom on the television. I could see the lead actor laughing.

HELP ME! I screamed, or at least I think I did. It felt like I did. My head was shoved back onto the carpet. I felt a cold hand palm my entire face, stopping the screams, stopping my breath. It covered my eyes with darkness. It pushed into my left socket. I could feel my left eye being crushed. Adrenaline was replaced by an odd serene release. I let go of the extreme, agonizing tightness in my muscles. I was sure I was dying. I didn't know how this was possible, why this was happening, or who was doing it, but it no longer mattered. This was the end.

I was pulled forcefully under the bed, where darkness engulfed me. I could feel the side of my face hit a cardboard corner; probably a shoebox. Just then, I felt like I was let go by all the hands at once. I was now falling. I was falling into nothing. It was pitch black. I was surrounded by pure silence.

I was moving fast, deeper and deeper into the darkness. I felt my hair whirling around my face. Hot air rushed by me, through me. A deep hopelessness and despair came over me. I was in such pain, I actually longed for the second I hit the bottom. Then light. The abyss became dimly lit. I saw hands of all shapes and sizes reaching toward me; clawing at me. I felt the nails of these hands tearing my flesh as I plummeted further and further down.

The will in me came rushing to the surface. I began screaming again. I felt it, and then I heard it. I could hear it. It was mixed with the cries and screams of others. I heard so many cries. It was an unbearable noise. It rushed my eardrums and made my ears feel like they were going to burst. I screamed even louder to drown it out. Then darkness. Just me. I was the only sound. I moved my hand. I could move my hand! I looked around.

The darkness gave way as I pulled the comforter off my face. I touched my ears. They felt fine. I snapped my fingers near each one to test my hearing. It was restored. I lifted my knees to my chest and sat firmly against the wall, surveying the room. Everything appeared to be in order. I looked to the television. The same actor appeared on the screen. It was the same episode I had seen a snippet of just a moment before the fall. The fall. I jumped up, now standing on the bed. I looked over each edge. I didn't see anything but carpet. I leapt off the bed, making sure there was a good four feet between me and the underside of my bed frame. I flipped the light on. Everything appeared normal. I ran my hands over my body. I felt sore on my side where I had been gripped by my ribs. I lifted my shirt and found a bruise forming on my side. I reluctantly bent down to my knees and lowered myself to the floor. I could see under the bed. There were a couple shoe boxes, and nothing else. I touched the side of my face, remembering my brush with a cardboard corner. Aside from the bruise, I seemed to be alright. I stood up. My body felt like mush. My muscles were reacting as if I'd just spent an hour on weights in the gym.

"Charlie," I said aloud. She wasn't in the room. I turned to find the bedroom door shut. I never shut the bedroom door.

I flew through the door into the living room. "Charlie," I called. "Charlie."

I ran to each light switch, illuminating the entire apartment. I didn't find her in the living room, and she wasn't in the bathroom or kitchen. I checked the laundry room, where her litter box was. No Charlie.

"Charlie!" I cried. I heard a rustling in the kitchen. I went toward the sound. I heard Charlie meowing. "I'm coming, Char," I assured her. I opened the cabinet door below the kitchen sink and found a fluffy face staring back at me. "How did you get in there?" I asked her as I scooped her up. I hugged her tightly and listened to her purr motor. I held her away from me for a moment and gave her a once over inspection. She was fine.

"How did you get in there?" She responded with a head butt to my chin and more loud, crackling purrs. "Well you seem okay." I kissed her head and put her on the cool, kitchen floor.

I spent the rest of the night on the couch, with all the lights on. I didn't trust that whatever had happened wouldn't happen again. I knew it had to be a terrible nightmare, but it seemed so real. I just couldn't talk myself into a rational explanation.

The next day, I decided to use Lauren's absence to my advantage. She had left to visit the set of a film one of her actors was working on. I scoured the internet looking for any logical explanations for what was happening to me. I wasn't getting very far with searches for things like *cabinets open by themselves* and *invisible person pulls you under bed.* I found a few things relating to ghosts, but nothing a sane person could buy into. Right? I decided to get more to the point. I typed in *shadow person.*

Shadow person garnered over one hundred fifty four million results. I was shocked that this seemed to be such a huge phenomenon. I clicked on link after link, hungry for anything that would give me peace of mind, yet what I found was the opposite. Some sites were purely informational, giving facts on reports of people who saw shadows that seemed to take a human or perhaps ghostly shape.

There were pages devoted to proving these occurrences were alien attacks by beings who had come to earth to study us or consume us. I found other sites that claimed the creatures were demons sent to devour our souls piece by piece, and when we were at our most vulnerable, drag us down into the depths of Hell. One blogger claimed they were harmless apparitions of ghosts who were having trouble passing on, and if we were willing, we should actively participate in their journey beyond. If that was the case, there was no way I was going to volunteer to actively participate in anything this thing had in mind. Some claimed they were angels. That certainly wasn't the image my head painted when I heard the word *angel.*

I then found something almost more disturbing than the aliens and the ghosts. The things I had experienced were symptomatic of certain psychological and physiological disorders. Fearing the worst, and feeling a need to find the most earthly, logical explanation possible, this seemed to be right on the money. I wasn't on any kind of medications, so I was definitely not reacting to a treatment. I didn't have sleep deprivation; at least not before this all started, so that seemed an unlikely cause. Then I found *sleep paralysis.* It was described as the circumstance in which a sleeping person might temporarily experience immobility. It occurs just as they are in the state between sleep and wakefulness, and it can feel as if they are completely incapable of using their limbs. This sleep paralysis can also be responsible for the types of hallucinations I was having. *Hallucinations. Great,* I thought, *now I'm crazy.* It could be for some people like living an actual nightmare. It feels totally real while it's happening, but in reality, it isn't happening at all. And it was possible that during these episodes, one might inadvertently hurt themselves, scratches, bruising, etc.

Well, it explained it. I didn't exactly like what it might be saying about me, but at least it wasn't nearly as nuts as ghosts, angels, demons, aliens, or other completely ridiculous otherworldly creatures. I then started surfing the web like a madwoman, intent on finding more about this sleep paralysis stuff. What I found ranged from completely disturbing to mostly tolerable. I decided that I wasn't suffering from a mental disorder like some, but that I was of, hopefully, some of the more mild cases, where it was being triggered by anxiety. I sure had a lot of that these days. I was anxious about the job, the move, making friends; possibly making a new boyfriend. There was a lot on my plate. That just had to be it. It didn't exactly explain the weird stuff happening outside my new bedroom, but I already had that reeled in as well. The cabinets were clearly the work of a mastermind mouse; the shower thing was caused by me not properly securing the light switch and my imagination running amuck, and as for the rest, well that's just it, I needed rest. I needed to do some breathing exercises and chill out. I was going to be just fine. Everything was just fine.

Shaken by my findings, and honestly a little paranoid I might be losing it, I decided a major distraction was in order. I asked Finch to join me for lunch, and we headed to the café down the street for a bite to eat.

"What's going on with you?" Finch asked, as he gently traced the back of my hand.

"It's nothing." I couldn't tell him what was going on. Or could I? It all seemed so crazy.

"Can't be nothing. You haven't touched your latte, and I'm pretty sure that means something..."

"It's silly," I said.

"Doubt it." He flashed me a grin. "Come on. Tell me."

"It's going to sound absolutely insane. I really just can't..." I couldn't believe I had even said that much.

"It can't be that batty. Seriously. What?"

My face scrunched up in protest. He was staring me down with his now obnoxiously gorgeous eyes.

"Fine. Ugh!" I snorted. "But you have to promise you won't run screaming outta here as soon as I tell you."

"Deal! Shake on it." He stuck out his hand and we shook. I couldn't help but laugh. He was really great at removing tension from situations.

"Alright, hmmm... where do I start? Do you think there's such thing as ghosts?"

"Sure." His response came so easily. I was surprised.

"Ok, well then maybe this won't sound so crazy."

"You're a ghost? You're not really here?" He laughed.

"No, not me," I said, laughing. "So either I belong in a padded cell and need medication, or my place is haunted by someone, or something... I don't know. There's been some stuff going on there."

"Like what? Like the hair thing? Mr. Ghosty?"

"Well, yeah, but there's other stuff, too. I've been having these sort of... nightmares..."

"Bad dreams don't exactly mean Casper is couch surfing in your apartment." He smiled and took a sip from his coffee.

"No, I know, I mean, they're like real. They don't feel like dreams..."

"I know what you mean. I have this recurring dream where I'm back at my high school, first day, and I don't know where any of my classes are. It feels super real. Freaks me out every time."

"Not like that really. They're sort of... violent." I didn't know if I should keep going.

"Oh. Hmmm..." He didn't know what to say. I had to switch gears.

"Then there's other stuff. The cabinets open in my kitchen all by themselves."

"Right. Mighty Mouse."

"Except, I haven't seen any evidence of a mouse anywhere, and I have a cat."

"Charlie doesn't strike me as the hunting type," Finch said. He was laughing again. The fact he was finding humor in this was sort of calming.

"Yeah. I guess that's true. Then there was this thing with the lights in the bathroom, and..."

"That's what the super is for. Call the leasing office. They'll get you fixed up. They might even be able to do something about that rodent problem."

"Okay. Yes." I agreed.

"So... about this ghost thing... do you think maybe you're just a little wigged out, living on your own for the first time and everything?" He had just hit on exactly what I'd been trying to tell myself.

"Probably. I guess I'm just not used to it yet." I hadn't told him about the sleep paralysis stuff or about anything I found online. It seemed silly now. I was relieved to have someone else help me with the logistics of what I was experiencing.

"Well, that's probably what's going on. I don't think you're nuts. It's totally normal to freak out. I was nervous when I first moved here. I didn't have ghosts out to get me, but then again, I had a roommate to help me cope with the *on my own* business. Just in case I'm wrong though, I think I should come over and do a thorough search of the premises; make sure there aren't any boogeymen hiding in your closet. Not to worry, I'm great at sniffing out the paranormal."

"Oh, good! My very own Scooby Doo." I smiled. I couldn't help it. He'd made it all seem so harmless and simple. "How about tonight? I'll grab a movie."

"Excellent! I'll bring a pizza!" He leaned over the tabletop and kissed me.

I worked through the rest of my day, feeling much better about my experiences. Finch was so reassuring, and best of all, he didn't think I was certifiable.

That night I came home to a completely tranquil apartment. Charlie was waiting for me at the door as usual, but all the cabinet doors were shut, and I didn't have any creepy feelings that someone was in the place with me. I straightened up a little and waited for my company to show up.

Finch arrived, pizza in hand, as promised.

"Before we eat, I should do a walk through," he said.

"You know, I'm pretty sure it's safe," I told him. "I haven't seen anything weird yet. I'm thinking they might have moved out."

"We can hope," he said. He squeezed my hand and went on a walk about.

He backed up to the wall by the bathroom and looked back at me, putting his finger to his lips. He crept toward the edge of the doorway and leapt around the other side, flipping the bathroom light on. He went inside and I heard the shower curtain fly back.

"Nothing in here!" his voice confirmed.

"Great!"

"Now, for the kitchen." He came back out and headed for the cabinets. For some reason, I held my breath as he opened each door. He peered into each cupboard, surveying them carefully with his eyes. "Not seeing anything here..."

"Wonderful. No mice. No ghosts. We're on a roll."

"Ah, yes, but I haven't seen your room yet."

"Be my guest," I said, motioning to the bedroom door. "Think I'm safer out here though. I'll let you go in alone."

"Good call." He went into the room. He checked behind the door and under the bed. I heard him slide open the closet door. "Whoa!" he said.

"What?" I felt a rush of nerves.

"There's something in here!"

"What?" I called again, not wanting to go toward the room.

"This!" He appeared from around the corner, a board game in his hands. "I love checkers! We have to play this! I haven't played since I was a kid."

I laughed. "Me either."

"Well," he said. "I didn't find any ghosts. I think we're all good here."

"Thank God." I went to the kitchen and grabbed plates from one of the cupboards.

We served ourselves up some pizza and settled in on the couch to watch the movie. A few slices and a couple hours later, we found ourselves playing checkers. We played twice, and each game only lasted about five minutes. It wasn't quite as involved as either of us had remembered.

"Well..." Finch said, after the board was packed up, "I had better get. We have work tomorrow."

"Yeah... work." I sighed.

"Right. Well, sleep tight. 'Rest assured; you and Charlie are safe now. If they hadn't moved on before, I think they definitely have now. I'm pretty intimidating."

"That's what I like about you," I said. I kissed him goodnight and we exchanged goodbyes. I locked up and glanced around my ghost-free living room. Charlie was sound asleep, snuggled into a fleece throw on the couch.

"Come on, Char," I said as I scooped her up and hauled her to the bedroom. She had no problem falling right back to sleep at the edge of the bed as I changed into my pajamas and found the right channel for us to dream to.

I woke up to the sound of a laugh track on a sitcom. I opened my eyes, but saw nothing. I could hear the television was on, but I saw no light, no glow, no colors, nothing. There was nothing in front of my eyes but pure darkness. I felt the air around me; it was thick and hot. I blinked my eyes rapidly, hoping something would change. Nothing. Darkness. Pitch black. I decided to go for the light, but as I went to sit up, my body felt very heavy. I wasn't going anywhere. I felt as if I were made of concrete. Then I realized, the pressure wasn't coming from inside me, it was on top of me. I was being weighed down by something else. I held my breath and listened. I heard breathing; not Charlie's, someone or something else's. Then I heard more. It wasn't just one breathing pattern I heard, but three, maybe four. I felt breath on me. Something was near my face, breathing onto my skin, into my eyes. My eyes dried each time the hot gusts of air hit them. I couldn't see anything. I screamed and kept screaming. I could hear it, it was audible this time. I was screaming, and trying to free myself. I felt every muscle in my body trying to work against this great weight, but I wasn't able to escape.

Then a sound came from the other side of the room. It was a hissing, gurgling, snarling voice. I heard it call to me,

"Ssssaaaaaraaaah." It choked out my name in such a disgusting way. It kept calling me. The voice came closer and closer. I stopped screaming just long enough to try to listen, to try and determine where it was. I heard something slide down the wall nearest me. It was now on the floor. It was dragging across the carpet, toward my bed, hissing and spitting my name.

I heard whispers come from the others that held me. I couldn't make out what they were saying. I couldn't tell if they were even making full words, but they were communicating with each other. The bed tipped on my left side. The thing from the wall had made it to me. I then felt a searing pain on my left arm. It felt like there were several tiny bars burning into my flesh. Then I was sure of it. I smelled my own flesh burning. I continued screaming, but now no sound. No sound, no sight. Nothing but the pain. I felt the lining of my throat tearing as I called for help, as I screamed for my life. I choked on my tears and my screams. I felt the same burning sensation on my other arm and then my hands. The heat in the room became unbearable.

I then felt thrashing over me. The creatures were moving, biting at me, scratching. I wanted to fight them, but my arms and my legs just wouldn't move. I felt my skin being torn from my body. I could smell blood and burning tissue. The cuts were getting deeper. I could feel their claws or knives or whatever it was tearing through my skin, deep into my muscles. I was being carved and broken into pieces. At some point, I stopped screaming. I gave up. I had enough. My body, my mind, my heart couldn't take it anymore. I closed my weepy eyes tight. My body was being pulled down again, off the bed, onto the carpet. I was being dragged under the bed frame. I felt hooks under my ribs. I was being dragged by my rib cage. The pain was intense and halted my breath. I opened my eyes again, still nothing.

Sound came back to me, but the only sounds I could hear were the whispers. I still didn't know what they were saying. It didn't matter. And then I was falling. I was falling fast. I couldn't see them, but I imagined the hands I had seen the time before. I knew they were there. I didn't have to see them to know that.

And then I hit the bottom. I hit the ground with such force, the air was stolen from my lungs, and I became instantly aware of where each of my bones were and that they were likely shattered. Why wasn't I dead? Why could I feel all of this pain; all of this pure agony? In that moment I wished it would end. I wished for death.

Then light came back to me. I saw the glow of the television. I blinked my eyes several times as they adjusted to the dancing colors. I could move my head. I looked around. I was on my bedroom floor. I gasped for air. My ribs still reeled from the pressure of the hooks I had felt before. I touched them. I could touch them. My limbs were moveable again. I struggled with the moment, trying to determine where I was and what was real.

My foot was being licked. I jumped backwards and looked down. Charlie was sitting on the floor, tending to me. She seemed concerned. I snatched her up and held her tightly. I was glad she was alright. As I held my friend, my eyes searched the room, looking for any clues as to who was here with me, making sure they were gone. I didn't see anything out of the ordinary.

I stood up and carted Charlie to the living room with me, turning the light switches on as we went, illuminating the entire apartment, eliminating the shadows. I went to the bathroom. I could still feel pain in parts of my body that I remembered so vividly being assaulted just moments before. I lifted my shirt and looked at my ribs. There was now more bruising on my side. I noticed my arms. There were red marks like they'd been held under trickles of hot water. They were sensitive to the touch, but they weren't clearly burned through. I had multiple marks on my skin all over that appeared to be tiny scratches and bruises. It looked like I picked a fight with a leaf pile. Harmless in appearance, but I just couldn't fathom how the hell they got there unless some of this was real. It felt real. It felt incredibly and horrifyingly real. How did this happen? Was I crazy? Did I do this in my sleep? I wasn't going to count on it. I was out of there.

Charlie and I stayed up the rest of the night, searching listings for apartments on the internet. If I left this place, according to my lease agreement, I would lose my deposit; an expensive sacrifice, but at this point, it seemed completely worth it. Fortunately, I had enough in savings to put down a deposit on a new place and pay first and last, but that would be about it. Things would be tight if I made this decision, but what other choice did I have? And what would I tell people? It didn't matter. I had to do it.

I printed out the best finds, and the next morning I called into work, saying I had a last minute doctor's appointment, and I went on an apartment hunt. I found a comparable apartment in a nearby neighborhood and followed through on the paperwork then and there. I went back to my place and paid a visit to my leasing office, letting them know I was moving. I told them the new place was move-in ready, so I would be out of there as soon as I could get my stuff packed out. They were kind, but they did insist on keeping my deposit, which I knew they would. Luckily though, since I had given them a security deposit, plus first and last month's rent, they would be returning a prorated portion of my rent for the month, plus my last month's rent I wouldn't be using. I would get it back in about thirty days. Worth the wait, I figured. I had to get away from that place.

I went to work that afternoon. Lauren was annoyed by my being late, but seeing as how she thought I'd had a doctor's appointment and all, she got over it. I told Finch I had found a new place and enlisted his help to move. He was surprisingly happy to help. I told him I had tried to go to the super for the rodent stuff and they were terrible about helping me, and so on principle I had decided to take my business elsewhere. I said I found a deal that I couldn't pass up, and since it was closer to work, and the amenities were better, I just had to take it. I'm not sure he believed me, but he acted like he bought my lame story.

A couple days later, all of my stuff was resting comfortably in my new place. I had told my parents I was moving because I didn't feel at home there. They thought I was nuts and fairly irresponsible for jumping ship on my first place, but they also figured it was my money and my own insanely expensive mistake to make, so they trusted I'd figure it out.

Charlie seemed to like the new digs just fine. She supervised as I unpacked boxes. I was just about finished putting everything in its new place, when I remembered that I had gotten Charlie a housewarming gift. I found the bag from the pet store and pulled out a giant ball with a bell inside. I shook it and watched as her eyes grew wide and her whiskers pointed forward. She was super excited about her present. I tossed it for her, and she chased after it. She played with it for almost a full hour before retreating to the kitchen for dinner.

I finished up in the living room and headed to the bedroom to hang my clothes in the new closet. As I hung, I heard the toy in the living room jingling and bouncing off the walls.

"You must really like that ball, huh Charlie?" I said. I stepped back from the closet and turned toward the bed.

Charlie was sitting on the bedspread. My head tilted in confusion, and then I heard it again. The ball was jingling in the living room. I turned toward the doorway and looked out. I didn't see anything. The jingling stopped. I stepped out into the living room area. The ball was laying still on the floor.

I stepped carefully toward it and then picked it up. I studied it for a moment, and then I placed it back on the floor. I turned toward the kitchen area and looked on in horror as I noticed all the cupboard doors were wide open. I had not left them like this. Adrenaline shot through my body. I felt nauseas. My hands went instantly cold, and all of my skin tingled. I stood, frozen, thoughts swirling around my brain.

I felt pointy, cold fingers weave themselves into the top of my ponytail. It was here. There was no escape. It too had found a new home.

Cinnamon

At 3am I was really beginning to have second thoughts about the last glass of water before bed. I'd already been up twice to go to the bathroom, and by this third sleep interruption, I wasn't feeling so hot. You see, as a teenager, I never had to worry about weight. I took it all for granted. I was a hot cheerleader for crap sake. In my early twenties, I still didn't have to worry about it. I was hot and legal, and I could drink all night and eat whatever the hell I wanted at 4am and not worry about what it was going to do to me the next day. Now, it wasn't so easy. Eat a cheeseburger one day, see an extra three pounds the next. I'd been working my giant butt off for weeks to get back into shape, and I was almost there, so I was working especially hard at losing that last five pounds. It seemed to be taking for-fucking-ever and a day to come off. I was doing just about every damn thing I could think of to get rid of it. I took two green tea pills around eight and downed a glass of water; then just before bed, my genius, almost thirty ass decided to down one more glass. I wasn't feeling much like a genius by 3am though.

After my third toilet trip, I decided I might as well weigh in and see if this crazy ass plan was actually worth sleep deprivation. I opened the cabinet door below the sink and grabbed my trusty scale. I placed it carefully on the ground, making sure the needle was positioned exactly at zero; this makes a difference you know. Even the slightest jolt when it hits the floor can really set the whole thing off. I surveyed that zero for a good long twenty seconds. The needle was just slightly off to the right, which of course means that if I were to jump on the scale at that very moment, it would have said I weighed a ton more than I actually do. So I crouched down and adjusted the dial on the front of the scale until the needle lined up perfectly with the zero mark. I entertained the idea of adjusting a little further to the left than it should be, but I did not. In the spirit of honesty and of course dedication to my goal of reaching my hot ass high school weight by bikini season, I left the marker right on zero. I exhaled and took a look at myself in the mirror. I lifted my shirt just above my bellybutton and gave my body a once over.

Not bad, I thought. I turned sideways and took a glance at my side profile. Not gonna lie, I was sucking it in pretty hard, but I could really see a difference. I was sure the pills were working. My efforts were obviously paying off.

I stepped onto the scale very slowly and evenly so as not to tip it in one direction. That can make a real difference too, you know. You jump on that thing too fast, it'll add an extra twenty pounds. In the interest of maintaining accuracy, I slowly balanced myself on the scale and peeked down at the dial. *139.* One hundred thirty nine pounds! I was just four pounds away from my high school weight. According to my driver's license, I was fourteen pounds away, but that's neither here nor there. The pills were working! Before I went to bed that night I weighed in at one forty. Obviously all this pissing was doing something for me.

Super pleased with myself, I smiled, and then a yawn forced its way through me. I glanced in the mirror. My face was all kinds of red and puffy.

"Shit," I said under my breath. I was tired. Why the hell was I weighing myself at three in the morning?

Ridiculous. I realized this and bent down immediately to put the scale away and get my almost sexy ass to bed.

As I reached for the scale, a quarter sized fuzz ball ran across my hand. It was a SPIDER!

"Ahhhh!!!" I screamed uncontrollably and let out a really weird gasping noise I don't think I'd ever made before. It surprised me. And it seemed to surprise the spider too, because he stopped. He stopped, and I swear, he turned and looked right up at me, into my eyes. He sat, ready to pounce, right there on my bathroom floor. His disgusting, fuzzy brown body was sprawled into an unwelcoming shape on my pretty, pretty tile.

Our staring contest went on for what seemed like forever. I was frozen in fear. I just knew, if I looked away, he'd attack. I thought back to something I saw on TV once. *Never break eye contact*, I thought. *No, that's dogs you dumbass*. I talk to myself like this frequently. Anyway, there he was. He wasn't moving. You might think maybe I had scared him. No; not this little hooligan. He was staring me down. He meant business.

My eyes met the door. I thought about making a run for it. That's ridiculous, I know, but I have this sort of girlish aversion to spiders, and this thing was no regular spider, he had a fur coat, and fangs, and I'm pretty sure he was smirking at me. He made a slight move to the right where the door was, as if he was testing me. He knew I was going to go to the door. He knew...

I quickly looked around for other options. I could squish him. I could stomp him out. *Wait; bare feet*. That was out. I could grab a tissue and splatter him all over my pretty, pretty tile with my hand, but then I would have to get close to him. That was out too. I glanced at the sink, looking for weapons. Nothing. But then, a glimmer of hope. My eyes fixed themselves upon my air freshener can. It glistened in the light, calling out to me. My can of Cinnamon Delight was gonna fuck up this bug's night!

I made a quick move for the can and aimed swiftly, pressing down the top of the cap and dispensing cinnamon poison all over the fuzzy nightmare. I laughed and then let go of the trigger on the aerosol can as I watched him do nothing. I got him! He was dead!

I returned the can to its original location on the sink, taking my eyes off my adversary for just a moment. I felt a small pang of guilt as I turned back. Maybe he wasn't a bad spider. What if I had just killed a momma and now all of her baby spiders were going to starve to death because she wouldn't be home to feed them. Then I realized baby spiders *really* means *more* spiders in my house, and who the hell wants that? Stupid thought process, I know. I shook it off and turned back to the... *Wait?* I thought. *Where is he?*

He was gone. I looked very closely all around my feet. Sure he wasn't within stepping range, I carefully moved about the bathroom, searching for the little menace. He was nowhere to be found. I looked up at the ceiling; I checked the tub; I looked around the door jamb. No spider.

Panic took over. He was free, and he was pissed. I imagined him off somewhere, plotting his revenge. I didn't want to leave the bathroom until I was sure he was dead, but eventually, I had no choice. It was him, or my sleep, and I'd already missed enough.

I turned the light off and exited the bathroom in a rush, looking back into the darkness to ensure he wasn't tailing me.

Back in my room, I threw the light on for a moment. My cat found this extremely annoying and pulled his paws tight over his eyes.

"Sorry, Sir Mix A Lot", I apologized. I pulled the sheets back to make absolutely sure there wasn't a spider, or an army of spiders, waiting there for me to exact revenge for their brother.

I went back to the wall and shut off the light, then ran to my bed and leapt in, pulling the covers over me quickly. I don't know what it is about blankets, but they really do feel like shields from everything evil. Weird. It's just cloth.

Finally after about a half hour of fretting over my brush with death, I fell back to sleep. My dreams were invaded by visions of eight legged creatures and things crawling all over me. His eyes kept appearing; his eight creepy, reflective eyes, full of hate.

"Aaah!" I woke screaming as I felt something brush against my arm. I swept my opposite hand across it to make sure whatever was touching me was gone. It was Sir Mix A Lot. His tail was sweeping across my skin.

"Sorry, Mixy," I said. I sure was apologizing to him a lot; poor kitty.

I calmed myself and snuggled back into my covers. As I lay there, now almost fully relaxed, I realized my bladder was completely full again. I didn't want to go back into that bathroom. I didn't want to face that spider again. I decided that even if it didn't seem it, that cinnamon spray likely killed him. I'm sure it's not good for bugs. It does have some sort of chemical cocktail in it. He probably scampered off somewhere to die. I'd probably find a little spider skeleton one day and laugh about this whole thing.

I bravely raised myself from the bed and walked toward the bedroom door. My first instinct, chicken that I am, was to turn on the light, but I had already upset the cat so many times, I decided against it. I walked to the bathroom and flipped on the switch with a quickness. The light assaulted my eyes, and I had no choice but to let it. I forced my eyes to stay open and adjust so I could make a complete assessment of the situation before entering. I scanned the entire tiny room. No spider.

Relieved, I pulled down my pants and went to sit on the seat, but jolted right back up instead. *Of course! He's under the toilet seat!* I pulled my pj pants right back up and prepared myself for impending battle. I grabbed the spray from the countertop again and steadied myself. With the spray locked and loaded in one hand, I took my other hand and very slowly pushed the seat up. Once the seat was up, I jumped back. Nothing. No spider. I shook my head at my stupid self, put the spray down, fixed the seat, and took my place on the toilet.

Done, I washed my hands; I always wash my hands, always. I made a move for my hand towel. Just as I grabbed it, I felt an all too familiar feeling up my arm. It was legs, tiny ones, climbing and weaving through the tiny hairs on my skin. I looked at my arm in terror and watched as that spider made his way up and up. I took my free hand and brushed him off me, shaking my arms out in disgust and yelping. There he was. I had flung him into the sink. *Quick*! I thought to myself. *The water*! I went for the faucet, but he had seen it coming. He made a run for it and took off up the side of the basin and was making his way up the side of the wall when I grabbed the cinnamon spray and got him once again. I kid you not, he turned and gave me a look like "this isn't over" before he booked it and disappeared up under my mirror.

"Damn!" I exclaimed. I wasn't afraid anymore. I was mad. I searched all around the edges for that little ass hat, but came up with nothing.

Knowing he was trapped, I had a burst of inspiration. I sprayed all around the edges of the mirror with my trusty can of cinnamon. Then, realizing that this obviously didn't kill him the first two times, and likely wouldn't again, I racked my brain for other items I might have in the house. I ran to my kitchen. I say ran, more like skipped, it's not that far from the bathroom being that I live in a 650 square foot apartment. I ransacked the bellows of my sink, coming up with a mostly dead can of ant spray.

"Aha!" I announced as if I'd found the key to some great puzzle.

I bounced back to the bathroom proudly and began spraying around the edges of the mirror. It was just enough to make it once around.

"Got ya now, asshole!" I yelled at the mirror. I caught a glimpse of myself in the reflective glass and suddenly decided I had gotten a little too carried away for four thirty in the morning. I placed the near empty can on the counter next to my cinnamon spray and headed back for bed.

This time, I did not feel the need for a bed check. I was safe. I was secure. I killed that little shit for sure. I smiled to myself. *I may have even burned some calories doing all that*, I thought. This thought made my little tirade less crazy and more worth it. I fell asleep in no time.

About half an hour later, I woke to a familiar smell. At first I thought it was nice. It was friendly. It was welcoming. It was CINNAMON!!! My eyes opened wide. Terrified, I looked left to right, right to left. I couldn't see anything. It was too dark. The smell was getting stronger. He was getting closer. I pulled the covers up to my chin. I looked for Sir Mix A Lot. He was awake too. He was more alert than I was. He hissed at something in the dark and ran to save himself.

Traitor!!! I yelled in my head. I didn't say anything out loud. I didn't want the spider to know where I was, though I was sure Mr. Spider and his eight eyes already knew exactly where I was. I wanted to flee; I wanted to sit up and defend myself; I wanted to do a lot of things, but all I could do was lay still, hold my breath, and wait.

The smell grew nearer. My sheet was pulled all the way up to my chin. I felt something slight on my cheek. A tiny, fury foot perhaps? Then I felt the crawl. Eight feet. I can't say I felt each of them, but I knew they were there. He was on my face! He had come to do what I couldn't do to him. He had come to kill me. I couldn't stand it. I couldn't stay still. I began flailing about like a spaz and screaming like an idiot, such an idiot. All of a sudden, I was very aware that there was something foreign on my tongue. He was in my mouth!!! I tried to spit him out, but it seemed he wasn't going anywhere. I was in sheer panic. I didn't know what to do. He could have bitten my tongue, poisoning me with his spider toxins and kill me; he could have gone down my throat and made a billion spider webs inside my intestines; he could eat my tonsils and then move on and eat the rest of my insides. I had no choice. I promise you I didn't. I had to do it. I moved him with my tongue over to the right side of my mouth, and I clenched down. I instantly regretted this as the bitter acid from his spider body oozed onto my taste buds.

I ran to the bathroom, spit like crazy, and threw up uncontrollably for about three full minutes. There he was. His mangled body was now in the toilet. Proof that I had finally got him. I went to the sink and rinsed my mouth out countless times. I brushed my teeth twice and took four swigs of mouthwash. I checked my teeth and my tongue over in the mirror. No marks left by Mr. Spider. It had been a while since it had happened. I didn't feel poisoned or anaphylactic. I seemed ok. I looked into the toilet bowl. I hadn't flushed it yet because I wanted Mr. Spider right where I could see him until the entire ordeal was over. I saw the remains of what I'd thrown up, all except Mr. Spider. Panicked, I bent down to inspect the bowl. Obviously, I didn't touch it, but I couldn't see anything. No spider.

Feeling defeated, I flushed the toilet. I sat on the floor, back against the tub and let it all soak in for a moment. *He had to have been in the toilet, right?* Maybe he just settled to the bottom; or maybe, just maybe, he'd be back.

I got up after a long while and dragged myself to the sink. I pulled out my scale and weighed myself. *Nice.* I had lost another pound; two pounds over night. The peeing almost seemed worth it now, but the rest sure didn't.

I went into my living room and pulled back the window shade a little. It was still dark outside. I convinced myself I should probably give sleep another go. I let the shade fall back into place, and just before I turned around, that's when I smelled it.

Cinnamon!

The Change

Ezra carried the crate toward the dark house. *He could have at least left a light on this time*, Ezra thought to himself as he carefully made his way up the concrete steps. Ezra hated the night. The sunsets seemed to taunt him daily. These night deliveries were really all he had anymore. Since the change, he really had no choice but to continue them. He had to keep working to keep the family farm going. He had never imagined though that this would be how he would do it.

He arrived at the door and tapped it lightly with his foot. He didn't want to put the crate down; he didn't want to take any more time than necessary when making his drops. The door creaked open.

"How many?" a gruff voice asked him.

"You said six; you've got six," Ezra said matter-of-factly.

The man's arms came through the doorway to grab the small crate. The moonlight caught his skin as he stepped toward the night air. His skin looked paper thin. Ezra could see every purple vein running just below his pale coating.

"Is it fresh?"

Ezra groaned, annoyed. "Yes. You know it is."

"Good." The man placed the crate on a table beside the door and reached in his front pocket. He grabbed some bills and placed them in Ezra's hand.

"Thank you," Ezra said. He let the man shut the door before he turned to go back to his truck.

Ezra got in and waited for a moment before turning the key in the ignition. He stared at the house. He thought back to the summer before. He would normally reach this house just after sunrise on his milk route. The old man and woman inside were so friendly. Sometimes, she would even have treats in the morning for Ezra and his older brother to take back to the farm with them. But Ezra worked alone now, that woman was long gone, and the nice old man inside was just a shell of what he once was, doing what he had to do to survive.

Ezra sighed as he threw himself back to the present. He turned the key over and headed back home. As he made his way toward the old dairy farm, his cell phone rang. He reached his hand toward the phone, which was sitting in the cup holder. He hit the green button on the screen and pressed the phone to his ear.

"Yeah," he answered.

"I need a delivery," the voice on the other end hissed.

"I'm done for the night. You should have put in your order earlier like everyone else." Ezra felt himself grow nervous. He knew he should be more careful when speaking with this customer.

"I neeeeed it. I'll pay double. Get me the usual. You have two hours."

The voice was gone. The call had ended. Ezra knew he didn't have a choice. He had to make one last delivery. He didn't have anything left in his truck bed. He would have to get back to the farm and fill up more containers to fill the order. He was really hoping Sadie was up for it.

He pulled the truck up to the barn, leaving the headlights on to light his way to the large sliding door. He slid the door open, and light fell out of the opening. He left the lights on at night for his girls. He thought it might be comforting considering the nights seemed to be darker these days. He didn't want them to feel like common barn animals. He caught Sadie's glare. She stared at him sleepily with her large eyes.

"I'm sorry Sadie. I need more, and it looks like you're up," he said, genuinely empathetic.

She shifted in her stall. She knew what this meant. She was exhausted, but she'd only been on the farm for a few weeks.

Ezra opened the door to her stall and grabbed a pair of surgical gloves from the table next to his new best girl.

"Alright," he said calmly, "let's get this over with."

"I can't give anymore," Sadie said.

"Yes you can. You have to. You know what might happen if we don't do this."

Sadie started to tear up. She thought about fighting it for a second but quickly gave up. She knew why she was there. She knew this had to be done for their own safety. She didn't have any other options at the moment.

Since the change, life as everyone knew it had been turned upside down. The initial invasion was swift and violent. They came as if from nowhere. They took over, turning a large number of people into creatures just like them. They didn't turn everyone though; they required humans for sustenance, and not all of them were killers. A lot of the ones that were turned by force, and even some that elected to change, maintained their moral compass and love for mankind from before the transition. In some places, none of the night walkers were murderous, which potentially posed a threat to their existence. In this sleepy town, that was mostly the case. An army of night walkers came and ravaged the town. The townspeople fought back. Ezra's family was instrumental in the resistance, but not all were lucky enough to survive it. Most were turned successfully. Some had bodies that couldn't handle the transition. They were too old, too young, or just too weak. The ones who fought back hard enough didn't seem worth the fight and were killed, like his mother and father.

It was chaos. In the midst of the battle, Ezra's house was raided by a group of outsiders. They quickly made it known they had no interest in Ezra. He wasn't sure why until he watched them drain the blood from his brother. Ezra's blood was less than desirable. He didn't even want it. As a child, he had suffered from a rare blood disease, causing hemophilia. His older brother was always strong and powerful, something he'd been jealous of until that moment. He would have given anything to trade places with him, to save him. They took him from the house before he saw the end. He didn't see his brother's life end the way he witnessed his mother and father killed. He had hope that his brother was still out there somewhere, but having not seen him in over a year, the hope was dimming. The dream their dad had for them of taking over the farm someday was dying more and more with each passing day.

"So, what do you say?" Ezra asked.

"What choice do I have?" Sadie answered.

"That's the spirit." He smiled. He felt guilty. He hated doing this, but he kept telling himself it was the only way. If he could buy some time, if he could keep *them* happy, he might one day find his brother.

He grabbed a new butterfly needle and hooked up a tube and a bag. He had just gotten new supplies from the hospital. The hospital had long shut down, so he figured it wasn't stealing so much as scavenging... surviving.

He took one of Sadie's arms and cleaned the inside bend with an iodine swab.

"Where did you learn to do this?" she asked, almost sounding friendly.

"Let's just say blood has always meant something to me."

"Okay... so you just taught yourself?"

"No. I was kind of sick as a kid, so I sort of took an interest in these kinds of things."

"You're not sick anymore?" she asked.

He sighed and tried to avoid the question. "I took off a couple years back. 'Went to college. 'Studied phlebotomy. I wanted to live in the city; be something. I guess this country boy just couldn't stay away."

"Really?" She winced as Ezra stuck the needle into her vein.

"I was doing alright, but the farm wasn't doing all that well, so I decided to come back."

"Yeah, just in time. Look where we are now." She glanced down to see her blood trailing from the tube down into the bag, filling it with her life source. She turned away.

"It could be worse," Ezra said.

"Oh yeah? I'm living in a barn, paying rent in blood. Everyone I know is either dead or one of them. Hell has joined us on Earth. How could it possibly be any worse?"

"You could be dead."

"A welcome change."

"You don't mean that." Ezra looked at her warmly.

Sadie tried to remain angry. She resisted looking directly into his eyes. It was over if she did. She knew he was trying to do the best he could. She knew that even holed up in this barn, things could be much worse. Before this, she was drifting from town to town just trying to stay alive. She had no one but the two near strangers she had come here with. They were alone and starving. At least here, they had food and some stability; circumstances notwithstanding.

81

"Alright. This one is going pretty fast. 'Shouldn't be too long." Ezra snapped his gloves off and stood up.

"Hey!" A voice came from the stall over. "You think we could come to the house for a shower?"

"Sure." Ezra headed over to the stall next to Sadie's and motioned for the two women, Jessica and Dani, to come with him. They got up from the cots they were sitting on and followed him toward the main doors. He had made a decent living quarters for them in the barn. There were five all together. He'd found some of them, and some of them found him. They were all in need of shelter, and Ezra was in need of a fresh blood supply. It seemed to work, for now. Originally there were seven in the group. There were two men who had come with Jessica and Dani, but they left one night and never returned. Sadie had come to the farm with two other young women she'd met on the road. He didn't know much about their story besides that.

He turned back to Sadie. "I'll be back in a minute. Just try and relax. It'll be over in no time."

Ezra allowed the ladies to take over the upstairs of his home while he prepared food for his barn tenants. He made Sadie a little extra. She'd been through more than usual today, and she needed the extra protein. He also grabbed iron tablets and multi vitamins for everyone from the cabinet. He shook out five iron tabs into his hand, noticing there wasn't much left in the bottle. He made a mental note to add it to his grocery list.

To conserve water, there was a four minute shower rule. Dani and Jessica made their way back down the stairs within 20 minutes.

"We have some laundry," Jessica said.

"Alright," Ezra replied. "Leave it in the laundry room. We'll make sure we get everyone's clothes tonight and we'll run 'em."

"Thanks." Jessica took the lump of clothing to the laundry room and paced it into a half full basket.

"Here," Dani said, moving toward Ezra. "Let me help with that."

He handed her a coupe plates and some paper towels. Jessica came in behind them and grabbed the water pitcher and a few cups. The trio headed for the front door. As they reached the screen, a loud scream came from the barn.

"Ezra! Ezra!" the voice cried.

"Sadie!" Ezra yelled back. He instinctively dropped the food, grabbed his shotgun from inside the door, and ran for the barn.

When he entered the barn he found a strange man, writhing on the ground on all fours, trying to make his way to the girl attached to the tube in the stall.

"Get back!" Ezra yelled at the man, pointing the shotgun at his sweaty head. The man's body was thin. His bones appeared to twist as he clawed through the dirt. "I said, get back. I will shoot you."

"Do it," the man said, choking on his spittle. "Please, do it."

Ezra lowered the shotgun. His heart fell into his stomach, and he felt the air leave his chest.

"Lucas?" Ezra managed to get the name out. He stared at the twisted creature in front of him, trying to make sense of what was happening.

The man carefully and slowly turned himself over. He was pale, almost blue. He was clearly malnourished. His face showed every bone, and his eyes seemed to disappear back into their sockets.

Ezra could feel his eyes begin to well. It was Lucas. It was his brother. He looked almost nothing like he did the last night they were together, but it was him.

"Lucas!" Ezra dropped to the ground to help his brother.

"No, Ezra, don't," he begged. Ezra didn't listen. He helped Lucas to a milking stool and propped him against a stall door. Sadie looked on in shock, silent.

"Lucas, what happened to you?" He inspected his brother. His body was stone cold. His color was that of a corpse. He knew this look well. More than half the remaining townspeople had the same characteristics. They were regulars on his delivery route. Yet none of them looked this ill.

"They took me, Ezra," he said. "But I'm home. I'm finally home." His head was bobbing. He was fighting to stay alert.

"Who took you? Who did this to you? What can I do? What do you need?" He knew the series of questions was impossible to answer right now, but he couldn't help string them all out at once.

He knew what his brother needed. He needed to feed.

"Hang in, Luke. I will fix this. Hang in." Ezra ran to Sadie. She was shaking, making the disconnect a little difficult. "Sadie," he said to her, "it's okay. He's my brother."

"He's one of them," she whispered.

"No," Ezra said, though he knew it was true. "I mean, maybe, for now. But there has to be a way."

She stared at him, confused. He wrapped her arm and hurried the bag over to his brother. He cut the top to provide a spout.

"No," Lucas hissed. "No, Ezra, I won't do it." He tried to push the bag away, but he was too weak.

"Take it!" Ezra ordered.

"I won't," he said.

"You're going to." Ezra used his forearm to steady Lucas against the wall and forced the top of the bag into his mouth.

Lucas choked on the first drink but then started taking larger and larger gulps. Soon, his hand found its way to the side of the bag and he was tipping it up towards the rafters as he squeezed the plastic to get the last drops out.

He had regained normal mobility in his arms, but he was still unwell.

"More," Ezra said. "I can get you more." He turned and looked to Dani and Jessica, who looked on in horror.

"No," Lucas said. "No. Not tonight. Can you take me home?"

"Yeah." Ezra helped Lucas up, and they went to the barn doors. He turned back as much as he could while still supporting Lucas. "I hope you'll all still be here in the morning. Please stay. Please." He turned back, and he and Lucas hobbled off for the house.

Ezra managed to get Lucas up the stairs and into his bed, inside his untouched room.

"We'll figure this out, brother. Don't worry," Ezra said. Lucas grabbed Ezra's hand, gripping it tightly. He drifted quickly to sleep.

Ezra left the room, full of emotion; full of questions. He shut the door. He felt torn between the memories of the brother he knew and the loyalty he felt toward the people in the barn. He wanted to protect everyone, and though he was sure Lucas wouldn't hurt anyone, he couldn't be sure the monster inside Lucas wouldn't. He booby trapped Lucas's door, quietly setting noisemaking objects all around. If Lucas tried to leave his room, Ezra would know it.

He went to bed, praying that in the morning he would have answers and solutions. He prayed that his brother would somehow fight this off and wake up normal again. And he prayed that his new friends in the barn would still trust him and continue to help him buy time while they navigated this scary new world together.

He then remembered the phone call he got before he had returned home from his deliveries. The last request was never fulfilled. Lucas had received the blood that was meant for Ezra's most demanding customer, Mr. White. Before the change, Mr. White was already feared and loathed by most. He owned nearly everything and everyone in the town. It seemed the only business he hadn't quite been able to buy or at least control was the small dairy farm belonging to Ezra's family. Ezra's father never had a kind word to say of Mr. White. They were always at odds. Mr. White initially tried to charm the family into allowing him to buy into the farm and gain control. When that didn't work, he resorted to threatening to crush them and run them out of business. He never had gotten the best of the farm, but it wasn't for lack of trying.

Now, in a twist of fate, Mr. White had become dependent on the farm. If he didn't want to kill for himself, he had to keep a supply of fresh blood on hand, and Ezra was the only game in town. Ezra was pretty sure though that there was an ulterior motive. He often wondered if Mr. White just used the service as a way to keep tabs on Ezra's business, or maybe he was trying to stay under Ezra's skin by running him around at odd hours, always waiting until the very last minute to place an order. He wasn't sure, but he did know that being the vial creature Mr. White was before this all happened, he wouldn't be the type to be shy about taking someone's life to sustain his own. He was scary then, and even more so now that he was seemingly invincible. Ezra tried not to, but he really couldn't help but feel intimidated by Mr. White. Every time he made a delivery, part of him wondered if it might be his last. He may not have wanted

Ezra's tainted blood, but what was to stop Mr. White from killing him?

In the morning, Ezra woke with a start. He leapt from his bed and tumbled out into the hallway to find the things he'd placed outside his brother's door unmoved. He carefully removed the things from the doorway and turned the knob. He was careful with the door. He didn't know what sate Lucas would be in. He found the room dark, shades still drawn tight. Lucas was lying in bed. Ezra went slowly toward the bed and leaned in. Lucas was asleep. Ezra smiled, happy his brother was home and happy he had made it through the night. Then he remembered his brother's condition. He wasn't exactly the same old Lucas anymore. He'd been turned. Ezra's stomach felt uncomfortable and full, a side effect of his extreme anxiety.

"You didn't have to do that," Lucas said, starling Ezra.

"What?"

"The door, Ez. You didn't have to do that to the door."

"I didn't know if... I mean I couldn't be sure that..." Ezra didn't know what to say.

"I know," Lucas said. "I don't blame you. I just want you to know, I'm not like that. I didn't want this." His pale face contorted. He was tearing up.

"It's alright. I know, Luke. I know. We'll find a way to fix this. There has to be something."

"There isn't," Lucas said. He couldn't help the tear that fell.

Ezra gasped as he noticed the small trail of blood coming from his brother's eye.

"Oh, it's fine. This is my new normal," Lucas said. "I need to rest for a while. I won't be able to go out until nightfall."

"Okay," Ezra said. "I'll let you sleep. I'll be back tonight. Need anything?"

"No. No. I'll see you tonight."

Lucas looked better than he had the night before. His face was fuller, and his eyes were sharper, brighter than they were in the barn. Ezra left the room and shut the door behind him.

Ezra went back to his room to get properly dressed. He went downstairs and made a large pot of coffee. He poured it into a handful of mugs, hopeful that no one had left in the night. He placed the mugs onto a tray and walked out toward the barn. The large barn door was open, so he didn't have to fight to slide it open with his hands full. He walked in and saw Sadie sitting on a hay bale, reading.

"Good morning," Ezra greeted her. He put the tray down on a bale next to her and handed her a mug.

"Thank you." She took a sip and exhaled loudly. She had a strange look on her face.

Ezra already knew. The others didn't come for their coffee.

"All of them?" he asked.

Sadie nodded her head.

"Why didn't you go with them?"

"I like my odds better here. There's only one of them on the farm, but there's hundreds out there," Sadie answered. She smiled.

"You didn't have to stay," he said. "You can still go. I wouldn't blame you. Lucas though, he's my brother. I know he's not like the rest of them. We can trust him."

"They say they can't be let around regular people for long periods of time; even the kinder ones eventually end up killing. I've seen it."

"Not Lucas. No way. You'll see." Ezra put a comforting hand on Sadie's forearm. She seemed to melt into it. Her face softened and she looked at him longingly. Ezra saw a brief, telling look that explained everything. She had feelings for him.

Her face changed back to indifference, and she pulled her arm away.

"Yeah," she said, "well, he better just keep to himself, you know."

"He will." Ezra was disappointed that she didn't allow herself to open up more, but he didn't think it was the right time to press it. "So, I guess I have some extra coffee. You feel like getting super amped up and helping me with some stuff around here?"

"I guess," she said. She took a second cup and they sat in silence for a few minutes, drinking coffee together.

After coffee, the pair went and fed the twelve Holstein cows and gave grain to the two horses. They then went and gathered eggs from the laying hens and took them to the house. When they got inside, Sadie paused for a moment in the doorway. She glared at the top of the staircase.

"It's fine," Ezra said. "Promise. He's sleeping."

Sadie shook it off and followed Ezra into the kitchen. She helped him rinse the eggs.

"Breakfast?" he said.

"Sure."

He made scrambled eggs and toast, one of the four dishes he was actually good at. They sat at the dining room table and ate together.

"I've never actually eaten in the house before," Sadie said.

"Huh. I guess you haven't, have you?"

"No. I kind of like it." Her face was soft again. The light from the window glowed through her red hair. It looked as if it was on fire around her face. Ezra couldn't help but stare. She was really beautiful. "What?" she asked, noticing him staring. "Is there food on my face?"

"No." he laughed. "You're just really pretty." He instantly felt like a moron. They both blushed. The energy at the table shifted. "Sorry," he said, "I didn't mean to..."

"It's ok," she cut in. "I mean, thank you." Sadie accepted the compliment and smiled to herself. She kept on with her eggs. They sat in silence for several minutes, neither sure what to say, but both enjoying their morning together.

After breakfast, Ezra went to the laundry room to start a wash cycle. He noticed Dani and Jessica's clothes were gone. He was worried about them. He knew he'd likely never see them again, and he wanted them to be safe.

"We can't worry about them anymore," Sadie said, entering the room. She picked up on his mood. "They're strong. They'll be okay," she continued. She said it with conviction, yet neither of them really entirely believed it.

"You're right," he said. "Well, they know where we are if they want to come back. Do you have stuff to wash?"

"Yeah. I'll go grab it."

She was only gone about two minutes. She returned with her knapsack. She only had a few things. She emptied it on top off the washer.

"What are you going to do now?" she asked Ezra.

"Well, I think I'm going to start a load of laundry."

"No, I mean the farm. What are you going to do?" She looked genuinely concerned. "You still have me, but I'm not really going to be able to...."

"It's okay," Ezra said. "We'll figure something out."

"But what about *them*? They're not going to go away. What happens if we can't keep them in supply?"

There was a moment of silence. They both knew what would happen. Even the meekest would be forced out of their homes and into the streets, searching for nourishment.

"We'll figure it out. Don't worry. Last night's deliveries bought us a few days. Who knows, maybe the others will come back. Maybe we can enlist a few of the normals from town."

"They're afraid," Sadie said. "There aren't many *normals* left. What if they won't help?"

"Then, we'll figure out something else." He was trying to sound cool and collected, but he knew it was only a matter of time before all hell broke loose.

There were seventeen houses on his blood route. There were only a handful of people left in town who hadn't been through the change yet. They worked during the day, managing the grocery store and the only gas station left in business, and they boarded themselves up at nightfall when it was no longer safe to be out. The town was small enough before the change, but after, most of it had either been killed or experienced a turn. Ezra didn't know firsthand what the rest of the world was experiencing, but from the stories he'd heard from the drifters he'd given shelter to in the barn, including Sadie, things were grim. There was a movement to coexist, but some areas weren't able to make it work. A lot of towns were completely taken over, and all the normals had already been captured and kept to be continuously drained, had been turned or killed, or had run to find hope elsewhere. With creatures like Mr. White out there, normals didn't stand much chance anymore.

Sadie and Ezra spent the rest of the day tending to chores around the property. As they worked, they got to know each other better.

Sadie, as it turned out, wasn't always so tough. When the change first came, Sadie was just an eighteen year old high school senior, with a world of possibility on the horizon. It all seemed to come crashing down over night. The town she came from quickly went under. There were shelters set up for people who had lost their homes due to the rioting and violence that occurred in protest of the takeover. She and her family were staying in one when it got invaded. In the hustle to escape, they were separated. She hadn't seen her little brother or her parents since, and she too kept hope that she'd one day find them.

She was forced to fend for herself. She had joined with a familiar group from the shelter at first. They set up a camp in the woods close to the town they'd fled, so they could search for their friends and family; but none were ever found, and the group began to lose members. Some were taken in the night. Others left on search and gather missions and never returned. When the group of sixteen became a group of four, and it became apparent their loved ones might no longer be in the area, they decided to move on. The four stuck closely together. They found a home a few towns away that hadn't been taken over. They were taken in by a nice elderly couple, who didn't mind the company.

They stayed with them for a few months, but it didn't last. The couple decided to invite the change. Two of the remaining group members had given up and joined them, and that left Sadie and the final member, Ben, on their own. They left in the daylight, taking one of the cars from the home. They were back on the road, traveling during the day, hiding out at night. They found two young women in an abandoned rail yard and invited them to travel with them. The four of them had made it almost another month together before Ben was killed by another traveler. The group found a man walking down the highway in the dead heat. They pulled over to offer him a ride, and instead, the man pulled a gun and forced everyone out of the car. Ben tried to defend the group and the car, and the man shot and killed him before driving away.

The girls decided to keep off the highway and travel through the woods. The three of them eventually came upon the farm, where they found Jessica and Dani, two other travelers taking shelter in exchange for peace keeping blood for the town's turned. They agreed to give what they could and settled in to their new home. Sadie relayed all of this to Ezra, trying to keep her emotions at bay.

"I really thought we'd finally found a place to stand still for a minute, you know," she said.

"You have," Ezra assured her. "You can stay as long as you want. On that note, you're all alone out there now, and I would feel better if you moved inside."

"I don't know," she said, looking up to the ceiling.

"You don't have to worry about Lucas. Look, it's almost dark. We'll sit down with him soon, and you'll see, it's perfectly safe." He had almost convinced himself this was true. He knew how vicious the turned could be, yet he knew there was no way Lucas could have lost his goodness, his heart.

"I guess we could try it. 'Beats sleeping in dirt.'" She laughed. She wanted to make sure he knew she was joking. She was incredibly grateful for all he'd done for her and the others.

They quietly prepared dinner together. There was little conversation as they ate. They were nervous as they awaited the sunset. When the food was eaten, the dishes were done, and the sun was finally down, they made their way slowly up the stairs.

When they arrived at Lucas' door, Ezra knocked before entering. Lucas was sitting on the window sill, looking out into the night.

"I used to love the night sky," he said. "I could stare at it for hours. But that was before it was all I could see. Now it just looks like death."

Sadie and Ezra walked closer.

"Are you hungry?" Sadie asked timidly.

"Always," Lucas replied. "But don't worry. You're safe."

"Is that why you're so ill?" Ezra questioned.

"I refused to kill. I refused to feed. I couldn't do it anymore."

"Anymore?" Ezra felt a twist in his stomach again.

"At first, I didn't have a choice. The ones who took me, they were animals, Ez. They made me hunt with them. I was one of them. I know it was wrong, but at the time I was so hungry. It was all I could think about." His face was turned to the window pane. Ezra could see his and Sadie's reflection in the glass, but Lucas did not appear there.

"Luke, you did what you had to do." Ezra tried to console his brother, though none of them truly believed what he'd just said. "Who did this to you?"

"It was Mr. White." Lucas turned to face them. Rage took over his face.

"Mr. White?" Sadie asked. "Who's Mr. White?"

"He's a disgusting pig. A demon from Hell," Lucas said.

"He's a terrible person. Was a terrible person. Now he's one of them," Ezra explained to her.

"No," Lucas said, "he's worse. They tore me from my home, Ez; they killed Mom and Dad, and they left you here alone. When they took me outside, he was there. I could barely stand I was so weak from what they'd already done to me. He was there, on the porch, waiting. He made me drink his blood. He made me what I am. When I drank, I felt it. I felt all the hatred and the dark nothingness that his soul is made of. He's a monster."

"Do you think he turned the town? Most of them seem to promote peace; coexistence."

"No," Lucas explained, "I am pretty sure everyone he comes across he kills. He doesn't have the self-control to stop himself once he starts. I was different. We were different. It was revenge. Mr. White was a welcomer. When the turned first came here, he took them in with arms wide open. They wouldn't have even known about the farm if he didn't tell them. He brought them here. He wanted us to suffer. He did this to us."

"How do you know all of this? Where did you go after? Mr. White is still here." Ezra could feel himself getting more and more worked up. His anger was overflowing.

"They took me with them. The others. They had a house in Shandon County they stayed in. At first, I was almost just like them. I had forgotten what or who I was before it all happened. I killed with them; I lived with them. They were my new family, until that day. That one day." A bloody tear came down the left side of his face.

"They brought home a child," Lucas continued. "He was maybe five, six. I don't know. He was so small. He didn't comprehend what was happening. They killed him, Ez. Right in front of me. I fought back to the surface. I remembered what right and wrong was. I fought off all that hate Mr. White had tainted my blood with, and I fought against what they were doing. It was too late for the boy, but I decided it wasn't too late for others. I quit feeding. I went on a hunger strike. I tried to reason with them. None would listen. I overheard them one night conspiring against me, so I made a choice to leave. Just as the sun was setting, I set the house on fire. I took my chances in the dwindling daylight, taking shelter in a shed nearby, and I watched it burn. I listened to the screams and the cries as they all felt their last moments, like so many of those we hurt. None of them made it out. They're all gone."

Sadie was crying, though she didn't seem aware of it. A quiet came over the room as the three of them soaked in what had just been shared.

"My God, Luke, none of this is your fault. It's White. It's all White." Ezra went toward Lucas.

"No, he may have provided the darkness that filled me, but I have to take responsibility for what happened. I was there." He wiped the blood from his cheek with a sleeve.

"We have to kill him," Sadie said. The men turned their attention to her. "Mr. White. We have to kill him."

"What?" Lucas said. "No. There's no way."

"No, she's right, Luke. He has to pay for this. We have to." Ezra stood up straight as his brain turned with angry thoughts and plans of violence.

"It won't solve anything," Lucas rebuffed.

"Maybe not, but it's a start," Ezra said. "The town is terrified, Luke. Even the ones who've turned are scared. They're scared of him; they're scared to be like him. This town will never be safe as long as he's here. And think about it, Mom and Dad are dead. They killed them. He was here. And look what he's done to you. You don't think that was personal?"

"I don't doubt that it was, Ez, but it's not going to change the world. We're already fucked."

"Fine, but it sure as hell will make me feel better. Help me or don't; I'm doing this." Ezra left the room, Sadie following close behind.

Ezra went down the stairs and found himself in the kitchen. He grabbed a bottle of whiskey his dad had placed above the fridge some time ago. He poured a glass for himself and took a swig.

"Can I get in on that?" Sadie asked.

"Me too," said Lucas as he appeared in the doorway.

"Sure. But can you?" Ezra grabbed two more glasses and poured two more drinks.

"I lost my appetite for burgers and fries, bro. I never lost my taste for a good drink." Lucas smiled a half smile. It was the first semblance of human hope he'd shown. "Besides little brother, you're not quite twenty one yet."

"I will be in September." He looked at Sadie, embarrassed. He then realized he was glad that his brother was even around to embarrass him, and he smiled. "Besides, I don't think the law applies these days. Do you see any kind of law enforcement here?"

The three laughed and clinked glasses. They powered down their glasses and opted for one more. Filling a third glass for good measure, they sat at the table for discussion.

"First things first," Sadie said, "I think we need to get Lucas some dinner." She looked at Ezra.

"Okay," Ezra said, "but you just drank a bunch of whiskey, and last night you gave quite a bit. I don't think it's safe."

"I want to. Look at him," she said.

Lucas was propped up in the dining room chair. His skin was almost transparent, and he was extremely thin and sickly. The fullness he'd gained in his face since feeding the night before was already starting to fade.

"No," Lucas said, "I'm fine."

"Nah, big brother. Let's get you something." Ezra patted Lucas on the back. "Come on, Sadie. Let's go to the barn."

Ezra and Sadie left their turned friend in the house and went to the barn.

"You're right," Sadie said while Ezra set up for the draw. "He's really cool."

"Told you," Ezra said. He had a worried look on his face.

"Don't worry," she said. She touched his arm lightly. "Hey, it'll be okay. Maybe someday we'll find a cure. And in the meantime, we'll just do this."

"You can't keep doing this. It's not safe. Now there's just one of you. And I can't give him mine."

"I know, but we'll figure it out. Right?" She used his words back on him

"Right," he said, exhaling. "Okay, let's do this." He prepped her arm with gloved hands and gently inserted the needle. He eyed the bag to make sure it was collecting alright. "Alright," he said, "just a little. Won't be long."

"Tell me more about your blood. Your illness. What is it?" she asked.

"Well, it's sort of hard to explain, but say I get a sizeable cut, or I have a needle put in my arm, it's a lot harder to stop the bleeding. I have hemophilia, which was caused by some sort of infection I had as a kid that led to this crazy blood disorder, and blah, blah, blah, long story short, I have been permanently deferred from the donor list."

"That sounds pretty awful. How do you keep from getting banged up around here?"

"I'm just really, really careful." He laughed.

"Yeah. I guess so."

They sat for about fifteen minutes while her blood flowed into the bag. At the end, as he was bandaging her arm, she reached up with her opposite arm and grabbed his shirt, pulling him closer to her. Sadie kissed Ezra. When their lips met, she almost immediately pulled back.

"Sorry," she said. "I don't know if it's the liquor, or the blood loss, or maybe the exhaustion..."

"Or you like me," he offered another option. "It's okay. I like you, I just didn't know if..."

"Yeah," she said.

They kissed again, this time longer. After a few minutes, Ezra moved away, remembering their current situation.

"We should get back inside," he said.

"Yes." She got up and followed him back to the house.

"Would you prefer a glass?" Ezra asked Lucas.

"Oh, funny. And yes I would. Thank you." His eyes dilated when he saw the blood bag. His pupils took over the entire eye. It took Sadie by surprise. "Sorry," he said, recognizing the expression. "I'm a little hungry. Thank you, for dinner." He didn't know what to say. It was very awkward, but it was appropriate.

"You're welcome?" she replied. She took a seat at the table across from Lucas.

Ezra brought the glass of warm blood to the table and set in front of his brother, who took it up into his hands and gulped it down. His mouth widened as it welcomed the glass. It was almost like watching a snake dislocate its jaw before swallowing a rodent. The two watched in awe as Lucas devoured the contents of the glass. When he was done, he almost instantly gained more energy. His skin became more luminescent, and his face again became fuller. His pupils returned to an almost usual size. It was a transformation unlike any other they'd seen.

"Quite the spectacle, huh?" Lucas said.

"It's just," Sadie choked out her words, "wow."

"So," Lucas said, "what is this? What are you doing here?" He pointed to the glass.

"I was keeping up the farm. I just changed up the product. Not everyone that's changed is like White. Some of them just want to get by, no killing. I provided a way."

"That's smart, Ez. That's real smart." Lucas put a cold hand on Ezra's shoulder.

"Yeah, well it was. We lost the rest of our blood supply last night. They all left." Ezra's chin went toward his chest.

"I'm sorry. I'm sure I had something to do with that," Lucas said.

"Yeah, well, I'd rather have you home." Ezra said. "Alright. Let's get to it. How do we get Mr. White?"

"Well," Sadie started, "Lucas said fire does it. We could burn his house down."

"He's too smart for that," Lucas said.

They sat in silence for several minutes, letting the wheels turn, searching for a solution. The phone rang, breaking their concentration. Sadie and Ezra jumped, startled by the sound. Ezra went to telephone on the wall and lifted the receiver.

"Hello," he answered.

"Oh, hello," the voice hissed. "So casual a greeting for someone so busy. You must be busy. You forgot something lasssst night."

Ezra waved his hand to signal the table. He pointed to the phone and mouthed *it's him.*

"Yeah, well," Ezra said to the voice on the phone, "I ran out. I couldn't get anymore last night."

"Well, isn't that a shame? How about now? Do you have more now?"

"I can get it. Yeah. But it's gonna be difficult. Double right? You'll pay me double?" Ezra recalled their previous conversation. It was taking all the restraint he had not to lose control and scream into the phone.

"Well that dependssss. How soon can you get here?" His voice made Ezra's insides turn.

"I have to collect the product first. Maybe three hours."

"Make it two, and I'll pay triple," Mr. White said.

"I'll try." Ezra hung up the phone. He came back to the table and tried taking deep calming breaths. He knew he had to focus on the task at hand; the bigger picture. Soon, Mr. White would be a bad memory.

"Wait," Lucas said, "he buys from you? He's one of your... customers?"

"Yeah. He's one of my biggest customers."

"That's it, Ez!" Lucas shouted. "You deliver him your blood. We let him feed on you."

"What? No, he'll never drink it. He'll know."

"No, he won't. I'm one of them, and I can't tell the difference between the two of you. All I smell is warm, fresh blood beneath the skin. It's all the same until you drink."

"But when they came in here, those others, they knew; they avoided me."

"They knew because he warned them. The whole town knew about your illness, Ez."

"Will this kill him?" Sadie asked.

"No," Lucas said, thinking harder, "it won't. It won't kill him, but it will disorient him long enough for us to get him where we want him."

"But," Sadie protested, "what about the hemo whatever? Isn't this dangerous?"

"Shit," Lucas said. "She's right."

"No." Ezra stood up. "Let's do it. I'll do it." He went into the kitchen and opened up a drawer. "Here," he said, tossing a marker to Sadie.

"What's this for?"

"I can't stick myself. Come on." He went right out the door.

"No, no, no," she said as she ran after him. "I can't do it. I don't know how. I'll mess it up. I'll hurt you. Please, no. Maybe Lucas can."

"You can. I'll show you. It's fine. I'll walk you through it. I'll even mark it for you. It'll be alright." He turned toward her and looked her in the eye. "I trust you." He kissed her.

This gesture didn't make her feel any better about her abilities to complete a blood draw, but she now felt determined.

They set up in one of the stalls. Ezra hooked a tube to a butterfly needle on one end and set the bag up on the other. He placed the bag into a bucket next to the cot he'd be sitting on. He took off his work shirt and handed Sadie a band. He took a seat.

"Tie it tight, above the bicep," he instructed.

"Okay," she went to it. "Is that good?"

"Great," he said. He made a few tight fists and then felt the bend of his arm with his opposite hand. "Here," he said. "Mark here."

She took the marker and made a dot.

He then felt around some more to make sure he could feel which way the vein was running.

"Okay," he said, "the vein needs to be tapped here, right where the dot is, and it's running this way." He trailed his finger to indicate the direction. "That's the way the needle needs to point, okay?"

She looked terrified.

"You can do this," he said.

"Okay. Okay. I can do this," she said. She exhaled deep and shook out her limbs. She picked up the iodine and swabbed the inside of his arm just as he had done on her so many times before. The black dot from the permanent marker lightened, but remained.

"Alright," he said, "perfect. Now pick up that needle and pop the cap."

She did.

"Beautiful," he commented. He was trying to remain calm and use soothing tones so she would relax, but he was scared out of his mind. "Okay, so just like I showed you, it goes into where the dot is, and it needs to face this direction." He pointed to it again. "Now, when you poke it in, don't be too gentle, it has a bit to go through, but don't go too hard; we don't want it to go out the other side of the vein. And let's aim for getting about half the needle in."

"Oh, God," she said. She was almost in tears.

"It's okay, Sadie. I promise. You can do it."

Her gloved hands were shaking.

"Deep breaths. Take three deep breaths."

She did.

Her hands steadied. She shook her limbs out one more time and let out an anxious yelp. She turned to Ezra and just went for it. She placed the needle in his arm, right where he had told her. His eyes were shut tightly. He opened them after he felt it go in, and he looked down at the insertion. It was in. He didn't feel any abnormal pains. There was no blood coming from where the needle met the skin. It seemed a job well done. He exhaled in relief and looked to Sadie. She looked green. She was clearly holding her breath.

"Breathe," he said. "It's good. Look. It's good." He assured her.

She sucked in air.

"Shit that was scary," she said. "I just... wow."

"I know." Ezra laughed a little. He pumped his fist and looked down to the bag. It was filling normally. Everything looked as it should. "Grab that tape over there on the table and put a couple across the tube here to make sure it doesn't move."

Sadie carefully placed two strips of tape across the line, securing it to Ezra's skin.

They now just had to sit and wait. They passed the time telling nice stories of things they did before the change. They shared stories from their childhoods and talked about their dreams for the future and how drastically those had changed. Their future plans and high ambitions were now replaced by sheer hopes for survival and whether the future held any semblance of normalcy.

Before they knew it, the first bag was full.

"Okay," he said, "we need to attach a new bag."

"No," Sadie said, "I think that's enough."

"He'll be expecting at least two more," Ezra replied.

"Yeah, well, tonight he gets one."

He was feeling dizzy. He knew she was right. It wasn't safe for him to continue now. He might be able to give more later on, but at that moment, he was feeling weak.

"Okay," he said, "hand me that gauze, please." He took the gauze pad from her and held it in his free hand. "Now, I'm going to put this just over the needle head, and I need you to just bend down the arms on the sides there, and pull the needle straight out."

"Sure," she said shakily. "No problem.

She did as he said, and he applied pressure to the source as soon as the needle was freed from his arm. It throbbed. He held the gauze tight. He knew that if the bleeding didn't stop immediately, it might not stop at all. Sadie grabbed a bandage and helped Ezra wrap it tightly around his elbow.

"You okay?" she asked.

"Think so," he said. "Let's get back up to the house. We have more details to go over."

When they got back into the house, Lucas had already devised a plan. They reviewed and even practiced a little, and then they waited. For their plan to work, they had to wait a couple more hours. When they were ready, they loaded up in the truck. Lucas laid in the bed of the truck and Sadie positioned herself on the truck floor. As they approached the house, Ezra's nerves ran high. He was scared that his face would give them away. He was also worried that as soon as he saw Mr. White, he might try to rip his throat out with his bare hands.

"Just stay calm," Sadie said, sensing the tension.

"Got it."

The truck rolled up to the large estate. Ezra parked his truck in the paved driveway, and flipped off his lights.

"Well," he said, "I'll be right back." He checked to make sure his sleeve covered his bandaged arm. He stepped out of the pickup and moved around to the side of the truck as he always did. He grabbed the bag of blood from the crate in the back.

"Be careful, brother," Lucas whispered.

Ezra nodded very slightly and went down the driveway, toward the front steps. He took each step with care as he cradled the bag in his arm. He took in a deep breath and knocked on the large door. He heard a stirring from within the home. The door was opening.

"You're late," Mr. White said. "That's disappointing."

"Well, it was harder than I thought it would be," Ezra said flatly.

"What's this?" His serpent-like eyes met the bag. "Where's the rest?"

"This was all I could get. We lost a few people over there."

This news made Mr. White smile. He took pleasure in the fact that for once business was bad on the farm.

"Oh. So sorry to hear that," he said. "Maybe things will pick up." He laughed to himself.

"You better hope it does." Ezra leaned on the assumption that this was Mr. White's only form of sustenance, though he was sure it wasn't.

"Oh, I do. I do. All my besssst," he said. He reached for the bag and snatched it from Ezra. He handed him some bills. "Double it is then... just for the one..."

"Right." Ezra put the money in his shirt pocket and turned to leave.

"You know," the voice called after him, "too bad your brother isn't around to help. Seems you could use it. Shame. Shame."

Ezra paused. His heart rate rose. He knew better than to turn around. Mr. White would soon get his. He continued walking toward his truck. He heard the door close and lock behind him. He jumped in the pickup and started it up. He purposely turned his brights on as he backed out of the driveway. He knew it was juvenile, but he was angry.

He left the driveway and drove just around the corner. He cut the engine and hit the steering wheel hard with his fists. Sadie popped up in the seat next to him.

"Stop," she said as she rubbed his arm. "We'll get him."

Ezra calmed and knocked on the cab window behind him. Lucas climbed out of the back and got into the truck. They ran through the plan one more time and waited. They sat in anticipation for almost an hour. They then got out of the truck and snuck back toward Mr. White's home. They made their way to the side of the house. Lucas peeked into a window.

"I don't see anything," he reported.

They moved around toward the front of the home. Then they heard a series of crashes come from within. It sounded like he was thrashing around inside the house.

"He drank it," Lucas whispered. "Let's go."

They ran to the front door. It was locked. They went to a window on the side of the house and found it open. One by one they climbed into what looked to be the parlor. Ezra checked his watch. He held up his fingers to signal, they had about five minutes. They crouched and waited. The thrashing got worse. Then they heard wailing. Mr. White was in pain. Ezra reveled in the sound of it. He had a rope in his hand. He started preparing it.

The window behind them started to glow dimly with the young light of a new day. The thrashing subsided. Mr. White was slumped over the dining room table. Ezra held his fist in the air to signal the attack. He and Lucas hurried into the dining room and wrapped the rope around White's body, making sure his arms were made immobile. He came to while they were tying him, and he started throwing his body around. Lucas hugged him tightly, keeping him from freeing himself.

"Now!" Ezra shouted. "The door!"

Sadie ran for the front door. She turned the three bolts that secured it and flung it open.

The men wrangled Mr. White and managed to work him to the door way.

"I'm going to eat your soul," Mr. White said. His words slid into Ezra, fueling his anger even more.

"Not today," Ezra said. He and Lucas struggled to get Mr. White out onto the front steps of the house.

The brothers tackled him to the ground and held him down on the concrete. Mr. White managed to get his left arm loose, and he swiped a flailing arm at Ezra's sleeve. His bandage was pulled roughly, and it started to bleed.

"Ezra," Lucas said, noticing the blood.

"I'm fine!" Ezra yelled. He was able to secure the loose arm with his knee. He pulled the rope tighter, forcing White's arm still. He laid all of his body weight onto the creature. Ezra looked to the mountains in front of them. The sun peaked over the top. "Go!" he yelled to his brother. "Get inside!"

"No," Lucas said. "I'm finishing this. I'm not leaving you."

"I have it. Go!"

"You're all going to die, and your souls will spend an eternity being shredded to pieces," Mr. White threatened.

"Shut up!" Lucas yelled.

"I had such high hopes for you, boy."

Lucas placed a knee on Mr. White's throat. He laughed as he gurgled.

"Go!" Ezra begged of his brother. "Get back!"

Lucas looked behind him. The sun would be on him any second. He let go of his position and ran for the safety of the front hallway.

Ezra put every bit of strength he had into holding down the miserable Mr. White. Mr. White looked up at the sky, and for the first time, his face showed complete and utter fear. His eyes widened as he finally considered that this could be his final moment.

"This doesn't end with me," he said. "They'll come for you."

"Let them," Ezra said, staring straight into Mr. White's eyes.

The sun broke through over the mountain tops. It traveled up the sidewalk and landed directly on Mr. White's face. Ezra looked on as Mr. White's eye sockets filled with blood. His skin began to crack and wither. His body suddenly stopped fighting and Ezra leapt backwards. He put his hand to his arm, trying to slow the bleeding.

He watched on as Mr. White seemed to crack entirely. He let out a loud scream as his body began to turn to ash. Pieces of him started to move with the breeze. The screams stopped and the remaining pieces of his head fell to ash. His body fell beneath his clothes and the rope, which then lay crumpled on the walkway.

Ezra stood, squinting as the light hit his eyes. He stepped toward the ashes and kicked the pile with his feet. Ashes flew from the pant legs. This was all that was left of Mr. White.

Sadie ran to Ezra's side. She had a kitchen towel in her hand. She applied pressure to Ezra's arm and helped him into the house. She then searched the home for something to wrap his arm with. There was a sport bandage in the guest bathroom cabinet. Sadie hurriedly wrapped Ezra's arm, finally slowing the bleeding.

"Thank you," he said. She kissed him.

They locked up the doors and the windows, and they made sure the blinds were all closed. They got as comfortable as they could and waited until night fell again before leaving. A great justice had been served, but there wasn't much to celebrate. Lucas was still one of the afflicted.

Word soon spread of Mr. White's demise, and a surprising outpour of support came to the three at the farm. There were people, normals and the town's turned, lining up to help. Normals offered themselves as donors to the cause, helping the turned, especially Lucas, stay nourished and docile. They had more help around the farm than they'd ever dreamed, and they had made allies of the entire town.

They maintained the hope that one day there would be a cure for the infected. They prayed for a reversal of the change. There was no guarantee they would remain safe here; there was always the threat of outsiders. But for the time being, it was enough for them to be able to coexist; to find peace among the wreckage. Ezra, Lucas, and Sadie had built a new hope. A new vision of the future emerged, and for the first time in a long time, the future seemed bright.

ABOUT THE AUTHOR

Elizabeth Fields grew up in the small town of Los Alamos, California. Dreaming of the big city and bright lights, Elizabeth moved to Los Angeles at the age of 20 and found success as an actress and model. She has been working steadily in the entertainment industry, appearing on television and in film and magazines. At a very young age, Elizabeth found herself drawn to the written word. She is an avid reader and has enjoyed writing since childhood. She is known by her family and friends for her creative flare, and she has always said that there is nothing more exciting than putting your imagination to work. For more information on Elizabeth, please visit elizabethfields.net.

NOTE FROM THE AUTHOR

Thank you for reading *Still the Shadows*. I hope you enjoyed reading the stories as much as I enjoyed writing them. I am a huge fan of anything and everything horror. If you liked these, you might want to take a peek at my first horror collection, *Don't Let Them In*.

For more information about me and my other work, or if you'd like to contact me, please visit elizabethfields.net.

ALSO FROM ELIZABETH FIELDS

Horror
Don't Let Them In

Young Adult Fiction
Best Friends Forever
How I Spent My Summer Vacation

Now available in paperback and for Kindle.

elizabethfields.net